MW00874130

THE JACK REACHER CASES (COMPLETE BOOKS #13, #14 & #15)

DAN AMES

A MAN BORN FOR BATTLE

SET IN THE REACHER UNIVERSE
BY PERMISSION OF LEE CHILD

DAN AMES

USA TODAY BESTSELLING AUTHOR

A USA TODAY BESTSELLING BOOK

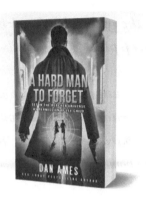

Book One in The JACK REACHER Cases

CLICK HERE TO BUY NOW

PRAISE FOR DAN AMES

"Packed to the gills with hard-hitting action and a non-stop plot." –Jacksonville News

"A fast-paced, unpredictable mystery with an engaging narrator and a rich cast of original supporting characters." –New York Times best-selling author Thomas Perry

"Dan Ames writes fast-paced, gripping tales that capture you from Page One and hold you enthralled till the last word. He brings a strong, clear voice to whichever genre he chooses. This guy is one hell of a storyteller. Watch for him." -Amazon Review

Dan Ames' writing reminds me of the great thriller writers -- lean, mean, no nonsense prose that gets straight to the point and keeps you turning those pages." –Robert Gregory Browne

These Jack Reacher stories are packed with action and unforgettable twists and turns. Great reads! -B & N Review

"Cuts like a knife." -Savannah Morning News

"Grabs you early on and doesn't let go." -Tom Schreck

"From its opening lines, Daniel S. Ames and his private eye novel DEAD WOOD recall early James Ellroy: a fresh attitude and voice and the heady rush of boundless yearning and ambition. Ames delivers a vivid evocation of time and place in a way that few debut authors achieve, nailing the essence of his chosen corner of high-tone Michigan. He also deftly dodges the pitfalls that make so much contemporary private detective fiction a mixed bag and nostalgia-freighted misfire. Ames' detective has family; he's steady. He's not another burned-out, booze-hound hanging on teeth and toenails to the world and smugly wallowing in his own ennui. This is the first new private eye novel in a long time that just swept me along for the ride. Ames is definitely

one to watch." — *Craig McDonald, Edgar-nominated author*

"Dan Ames pulls off a very difficult thing: he re-imagines what a hardboiled mystery can be, and does it with style, thrills and humor. This is the kind of book mystery readers are clamoring for, a fast-paced story with great heart and not a cliché to be found." -- *Jon A. Jackson, author of Badger Games*

"Dan Ames is a sensation among readers who love fast-paced thrillers." – *Mystery Tribune*

"A smart detective story stuffed with sharp prose and great action." –*Indie Reader*

NEW SERIES! JACK REACHER'S SPECIAL INVESTIGATORS.

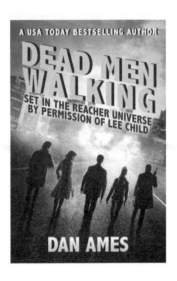

CLICK HERE TO BUY NOW!

FREE BOOKS AND MORE

**Would you like a FREE copy
of my story BULLET RIVER and the
chance
to win a free Kindle?**

**Then sign up for the DAN AMES BOOK
CLUB:**

For special offers and new releases, sign up here

THE JACK REACHER CASES (A MAN BORN FOR BATTLE)

by

Dan Ames

He who tells a lie is not sensible of how great a task he undertakes; for he must be forced to invent twenty more to maintain that one.

-Alexander Pope

CHAPTER ONE

They were known as the three sisters.

In a town as small as Gideon, Indiana, that kind of sobriquet wasn't totally unexpected; a small community often uses shorthand for local objects of interest and three dark-haired beauties were no exception.

As is so often the case in instances such as this, more than one reason for the trio's popularity existed. Of particular note was their likenesses which were so similar that many speculated they were triplets. They most certainly were not triplets; in fact, they weren't even sisters.

However, each of the three was strikingly beautiful. In fact, one older farmer remarked over a breakfast of scrambled eggs in the local diner that the three "sisters" could have made more money working as models in Paris. His dining companions nodded their heads in collective agreement.

Their means of income also had led to the nickname: they were owners of the Three Sisters Tire Company. The little auto repair shop had been a low-level affair for years and years, owned by a man whose main income was a welfare check and who only occasionally opened the doors to the little gas station that no longer sold gas.

The little white building with the garage sporting two full bays with retractable doors and auto hoists had occupied the corner of 4th Street and Elm for nearly eight years.

One day, instead of being called Sullivan Auto – which had been the original name until the welfare recipient somehow came to own it – the original sign was gone and in its place was a professionally painted logo: The Three Sisters Tire Company.

No one knew for sure how the sisters had managed to acquire the little business, and no one really cared. What mattered was that it was usually open and had tires just as good as the Walmart out on Highway 26. Most of the locals of Gideon, Indiana, shopped at the ugly mega retail store begrudgingly; they were on budgets, and the low prices helped out.

However, if push came to shove and they could find something from an actual local business —that didn't belong to a family of billionaires somewhere in Arkansas— at a competitive price, they'd give their business to a neighbor, who just might return the favor.

And so it was the little auto repair shop experienced a rebirth and soon, it wasn't uncommon to see both garage bays occupied by paying customers. The sisters didn't do the work themselves, they'd managed to lure a certified mechanic from Chicago – which was just a few hours away – and the man knew his cars.

Soon, talk at the local café was all about if and when the beautiful sisters might find some local boys worthy of entering into holy matrimony. The women didn't get out much and talk at the bowling alley over pitchers of beer speculated maybe they went to the big city on weekends.

It was pointed out they had half of a duplex apartment on Lincoln Street, just a few blocks from the tire shop, and they seemed to be home most of the time.

Talk of that quickly came to an end thanks to the same farmer who was fond of comparing the sisters to the most gorgeous supermodels on the covers of slick magazines down at the Piggly Wiggly.

Talk ended because one cool morning the farmer was driving into town for his daily coffee and eggs when he noticed three signs hanging down from the town's welcome arch that had been erected sometime in the 1950s when optimism and the community's municipal improvement budget were at an all-time high.

The farmer lightly pressed on the old Ford F-150's brake pedal and he slowed down.

As he came closer to the arch and the plaque off to the right welcoming visitors to "Gideon, Indiana, where happiness is always in bloom," the farmer realized they weren't signs.

They were three bodies.

Each hung by the neck.

The faces were twisted and distorted in ugly death grimaces, but the farmer recognized them straight off.

The three sisters.

CHAPTER TWO

"This is torture."

Tallon looked over at Pauling. She was doing some sort of bizarre pose dreamed up by the yoga instructor at the front of the class. It had some kind of animal name but Tallon figured it was all make-believe. The "instructor" was probably a con artist getting a huge kick out of people falling for a workout designed around pretending to be a jungle species.

"Shhhh," Pauling said.

He had to smile. Pauling was doing great. She'd been shot twice in a case that had taken her to Belize among other locations. Luckily, the bullets hadn't hit any major organs and she'd been able to recover quickly. Yoga was the final piece of the physical rehabilitation Pauling had endured without complaint for the past twelve weeks. From Tallon's perspective, she was doing great.

He, on the other hand, was drenched in sweat and praying the hand on the clock would move faster. His legs and arms were wobbly. Across from him, a woman in her sixties was rock steady and seemed to have a smug smile on her face as she watched Tallon struggle.

Mercifully, class ended less than five minutes later, and Tallon chugged from his water bottle and toweled the sweat off his face. The yoga studio was on the third floor of an old building in Lower Manhattan and the space was kept hot. Supposedly, the heat helped purge the body of toxins. All Tallon knew was he couldn't wait to get out of the damn sweat lodge.

"You looked a little shaky there," Pauling teased him. She had never looked more beautiful to Tallon: striking green eyes, blondeish hair with just a touch of highlights, and that great, whiskey-and-cigarette voice that always made him tingle in all the right places.

"Yeah, yoga's good for skinny little things like you," Tallon said, knowing how lame it sounded but going ahead with it anyway. "That's why you don't see a lot of guys built like me in here."

Pauling smiled but didn't take the bait. He understood why; he'd been trying to take part in her physical therapy when he could, so she didn't always feel like she was going through it alone. In the early stages it hadn't been possible but now she was close to one hundred percent.

They'd already been to the gun range several times and her shooting was back on point. They were pretty much equals on the range. One day he scored better, the next, she did.

They gathered their gear and left the yoga studio for the walk back to Pauling's place. The cool air felt amazing to Tallon and he begrudgingly admitted to himself that he felt great. Super relaxed. Maybe there actually was something to this yoga thing.

Pauling lived in a walkup on Barrow Street. Tallon had pretty much lived with her since the shootout and had helped take care of her as well as do the mundane tasks like grocery shopping and cooking.

He'd actually enjoyed the hell out of taking care of Pauling and in a way didn't want it to end. Even though they'd committed to each other and Pauling had sold her business and had been spending a lot of time at Tallon's ranch out West, they were still busy professionals. Especially

Tallon. He'd talked of slowing down, but it seemed there was always a new job in private security he couldn't turn down. He was fine financially, but it was always easy to imagine that just a little bit more would be great.

They made their way up to Pauling's loft-style apartment where she undid the alarm. Inside, Pauling went to shower while Tallon headed straight for the fridge and popped a cold beer.

Nothing like a cold beer after hot yoga, he thought and laughed. If his fellow special ops soldier friends knew he'd gotten his ass kicked in a yoga class, they would never let him hear the end of it.

Tallon went into the living room. It was a great space with huge windows that let in plenty of natural light. Pauling's style was contemporary but comfortable. Lots of natural wood, leather and original art.

As he thought of his comrades-in-arms ribbing him over his newfound interest in yoga, Tallon's cell phone buzzed and he glanced at the message.

Manuel "Manny" Ordonez. He and Tallon had fought side by side and had known each other for years.

Tallon looked at the text message.

It was simple, direct and pure Manny Ordonez.

Someone killed my sister. I need your help.

CHAPTER THREE

They called him La Roca, which in Spanish meant "The Rock."

It wasn't because he was a fan of the professional wrestler turned actor; rather, it had to do with his peculiar physiognomy.

As a kid, he'd had a tremendous underbite. His lower jaw had stuck out at least several inches farther than his upper. A group of physicians had toured his small village and offered to help. They'd manually broken his jaw, removed chunks on either side and bolted it all back together.

The operation had gone horribly wrong. An infection set in and parts of the bone began to fail. This required a second operation and the addition of metal plates and even more metal hardware to hold most of his jaw, face and even parts of his skull together.

He almost died on the operating table.

Twice.

Years later, after everything had healed and was as good as it was ever going to get, he'd gotten into a fistfight. His opponent had landed a good punch to the side of La Roca's face. The young man's hand broke in several places.

The boy who'd endured multiple surgeries and who'd been left with a severely misshapen head was fine.

As the fighter hopped around, howling in pain and holding his broken hand, he'd shouted: "It's like hitting a rock!"

The nickname had stuck.

He wasn't a big man, just under 5'7" but he was wide and powerfully built. His legs were especially short and his upper body oversized and muscular.

La Roca occasionally wore a black cowboy hat with a band made of Mexican rattlesnake. People opined he wore the hat to compensate for his overly large jaw, which jutted out like a block of granite, and to hide the dented and malformed skull. They were right. He felt the hat made him look more normal.

He had just arrived in the United States via an

underground tunnel. In the back of a panel van, he was driven north to Denver. There were two other men in the van, employees of the same organization that was paying La Roca for the task at hand.

Not much was said in the van. They'd given him identification papers and a gun. They also told him a car was ready with a full tank of gas and more weapons in the trunk.

When they reached Denver, they drove into the heart of the city to an underground parking garage. The van stopped and the men pointed toward a car.

"Keys are inside. Good luck," the man in the passenger seat said.

La Roca exited the van, started toward the car and then turned back to the panel van, as if he'd forgotten something.

He hadn't.

He shot both the driver and the passenger in the head, then pulled the van into an empty parking space. He tore a swath of cloth from the driver's shirt, popped the cap to the fuel tank and fed the cloth in. He pulled it back out and then put the other end of the cloth in and pushed it as far as it would go.

He went back to his car, backed it out of the

space and then opened the driver's door and left the engine running.

La Roca lit the piece of cloth, jogged back to his car and drove ahead. Just as he was about to turn the corner and exit the garage, he heard a loud *woomph* and felt the air vibrate around him.

He pulled out of the parking lot (there were no cameras – he'd made sure of that) and pointed the car, a big American Buick, toward somewhere he'd never heard of.

Gideon, Indiana.

CHAPTER FOUR

The girl was nervous.

Her friend wasn't.

The nervous girl's name was Tanya and she was fifteen years old. Her friend, Roquelle, was a year older but much wiser in the ways of the street. It had been her idea to come here, to this scary-looking motel on the edge of town. It seemed Roquelle had a date with an older man, a very *generous* older man, and wanted Tanya to ride shotgun, whatever that meant.

Now Roquelle pulled a half-pint bottle of peach-flavored vodka from her back pocket, took a drink, and handed the bottle to Tanya.

"Here, this will calm your nerves," Roquelle said. Tanya gulped the vodka and felt it burn her throat. She coughed and a little went up her nose, into her sinuses. Tears came to her eyes.

"Jesus, you're such a little bitch," Roquelle said, laughing. "You should be thanking me for bringing you here instead of cowering. Hell, you could walk away with a hundred bucks, maybe more."

"For doing what?"

Roquelle's eyes flattened. "Nothing you don't want to do."

Tanya noticed that Roquelle's eyes darted away from hers when she answered. People had told Tanya not to trust Roquelle, that she was bad news, but she didn't believe it. She thought the older girl was cool, tough and bold. The kind of person she, Tanya, wanted to be.

There was a knock on the room's door and Roquelle opened it.

A man stepped inside.

He was tall, with broad shoulders, sandy hair and blue eyes.

He shut the door behind him and stared at Roquelle, then glanced over her shoulder at Tanya.

"This is her?" he asked Roquelle.

Her friend turned to her but answered the man.

"Yes."

The man nodded, reached back and slid home the dead bolt on the door as well as the security chain.

"What's your name?" he asked her.

"Tanya." She paused, then added, "What's yours?"

His hands went to his belt. He unclasped the buckle and slid the long piece of leather from around his waist. He held it loose in his hands, like a whip.

"Call me Reacher," he said. "And then take off your clothes and get on the bed."

CHAPTER FIVE

Pauling's face darkened at the news. "Oh, no. I'm sorry, Michael," she told Tallon.

"Yeah, helluva thing," he said. The message had come out of nowhere and although he'd tried to call Manny, there wasn't an answer. Instead, Manny had sent an address in Indiana and asked Tallon to meet him there as soon as possible.

She watched as he slowly packed a bag. They'd spent most of the day in bed, knowing they'd be apart, but not knowing for how long. Their love-making had been gentle since Pauling's injuries but now, they'd thrown caution to the wind and let their passion and emotion take control.

Tallon was going to fly back to his ranch near

Death Valley, collect his vehicle and gear, and then drive to the small town in Indiana he'd never heard of: Gideon.

Pauling felt a strange sense of guilt. She'd needed Tallon during her recovery from the gunshot wounds and now it seemed like he was going off to help someone else. She knew he was on the verge of accepting a private security gig in Africa and wondered if another act of charity would prevent him from going. Secretly, she hoped it would. Pauling wanted him to scale back his military contracts, especially overseas in dangerous areas. She wanted this for purely selfish reasons.

"Does your friend not trust the police?" she asked him.

Tallon zipped up his single suitcase; traveling light was a habit of his.

"Probably not," he answered her. "Manny spent time in military security both in the service and out. He's a really sharp guy. Extremely organized. Highly motivated. Even if the local cops are good, Manny is better. No doubt in my mind."

Pauling knew he was right. "Maybe by the time you get there they'll have caught the people responsible."

Even as she said it, she was guessing it

wouldn't be true. If Manny was as good as Tallon said, he wouldn't have called his old buddy and asked for help. If Manny thought the cops were going to catch the guilty party, there would be no need for Tallon's services.

Pauling saw Tallon glance at his watch.

"Time to go if I'm going to make my flight," he said.

They embraced again and kissed. She felt his hands perhaps subconsciously touch the parts of her body where she'd been shot. It would be the first time since that gun battle she would be alone.

"Are you sure you're okay with me leaving?" he asked again. "I can call one of my other guys to go help Manny."

"He asked *you*," she said. "You need to go. And yes, I'll be fine."

He kissed her again. She looked into his blue eyes, saw the humor behind them.

"You need to come out West," he said. "Get some sunshine, you're looking kind of pale. Almost ghoulish."

Pauling pushed him toward the door and gave his butt a little smack. "Don't let the door hit you on the way out."

She was still laughing when she closed the

door. But the smile faded quickly as she faced the empty space.

Alone again, she thought.

CHAPTER SIX

She would have preferred to use the acronyms, but it sounded a little ridiculous. So instead of saying ISP (CID) she introduced herself as "Detective Pitts: Indiana State Police – Criminal Investigation Division."

The local Gideon cop, a big farm boy named Davenport, literally stepped back from her, as if her title had delivered some sort of physical affront. Using her full title was laborious, but it saved the time it would have taken for the local cop to figure out what it stood for.

She saw him look for a name tag and then back up at her.

Farm boy Davenport nodded. Pitts wondered when was the last time he'd seen a black woman up close and personal. Weeks? Months? Worse yet, she was his superior in this case, but so far, he seemed to be handling it okay.

The crime scene technicians had come and gone, except for the lead coroner, a man named Chang. His team had worked the scene thoroughly, photographing the victims, bagging any trace evidence they could find and mapping the crime scene.

Then, they'd removed the bodies of the three dead women who'd been hung from the welcome arch that spanned the road into Gideon, Indiana.

Pitts, or "Stevie" to her close friends, (her parents had been huge Stevie Wonder fans) had also worked the scene. She'd made notes, sketched the position of the bodies and tried to interview any witnesses she could find. All while trying not to get in the way of the crime scene techs. They were there to do a job, too and at times, working a crime scene was like a carefully choreographed dance – especially when it was done right.

For the time being she was here alone. Her partner had retired two weeks earlier and the brass back in Indianapolis were still trying to find a replacement. Pitts sort of enjoyed working solo, but knew she would need help on this one. This kind of case was going to blow up fast in the media if it wasn't solved quickly. Nothing got the bureaucracy of the ISP moving faster than bad press. Pitts had seen it time and time again.

Now, Chang, the lead coroner, approached her.

"First thoughts?" Pitts asked him. They'd rubbed shoulders a few times and Pitts knew Chang was good at what he did. He was a tiny man with an oval face and breath that always smelled like onions.

"The bodies were clean," he said. "No signs of a struggle or sexual assault."

"So more than one killer," Pitts intuited. "Unless it was one person who had put the fear of God into them and motivated them to follow orders without putting up a fight."

Chang put a tiny hand to his chin. "My guess is more than one perp. It would have been a rather elaborate process to hang three women from the bridge. Plus, speed would have been of the essence and this road sees a fair amount of traffic, even though the town is small."

"Any prints?"

"Maybe. A few partials near where the ropes were tied to the railing."

"Anything special about the rope?"

Chang shook his head. "Afraid not. But we'll

test the fibers and see if anything jumps out. Pretty clean overall, though. Whoever did this was highly organized and very thorough."

"Great," Pitts muttered.

Chang wished her luck, promised he would expedite the processing of the crime scene findings and then left.

Pitts stood and looked at the little arch. "Welcome to Gideon," it said.

"Hardly," she said to no one.

She walked back to her unmarked sedan and pointed it toward town. It was time to get some coffee and to find a hotel.

Pitts had a feeling she wouldn't be leaving this shithole any time soon.

CHAPTER SEVEN

The bar was not trendy. Instead, it was a neighborhood kind of place, not too far from the FBI's New York office just off of Lafayette in Lower Manhattan.

Pauling was the last to arrive as the others had come together directly from the job.

"We thought maybe we should bring you a vest," Agent Nicky Friselle said. Nicky was one of Pauling's last real friends still with the Bureau. She was a firecracker of a woman with short red hair and was usually dressed in a form-fitting black suit and whose favorite thing in the world was a black leather jacket. Nicky was a dogged investigator; her tenacious nature was legendary.

Pauling had finally accepted the invitation from her old coworkers to meet for a drink.

They'd visited her during her rehab and eventually, were aggressive in getting her out of her condo.

"A vest wouldn't have helped, but I appreciate the thought," Pauling said.

"Looking good, Pauling," Agent Roger Chinnock said. He was the youngest of the crew, tall and good-looking. Pauling had been partially responsible for his training and while he was very intelligent, he had a stubborn streak and it had taken some time for him to recognize the need for some degree of conformity at the Bureau. Their relationship had been rocky, but it seemed since she'd left hard feelings had all been forgotten.

"You too, Roger."

Now that Tallon had left to go help his friend Manny, Pauling had started to feel just a little bit sorry for herself. So when the invitation had come, she'd finally relented and agreed to the outing.

Pauling said hello to the others in the group: there was Agent Christina Paulette, a specialist in financial crimes, as well as Agent Bart Osgood, a year away from retirement and looking like he needed the rest.

They ordered drinks – sparkling water for

Pauling as she was still on a few medications to ensure an infection-free recovery.

They swapped stories and then Pauling asked them what they were up to, which was an oftentimes awkward turn of conversation. She knew they would have to be careful what they said, despite Pauling's history as an FBI agent. Talking about classified information was a sure way to abruptly end your career.

"Mostly dealing with our friends to the south," Nicky said. "What with the current administration's focus on illegal immigration, and the recent massacre of innocents, it's ramped up quite a bit."

The "massacre" Nicky referred to, Pauling knew, was that of a group of American families who'd been slaughtered en masse traveling to Mexico City. No one knew if it was a planned hit or simply a case of mistaken identity.

"We call them the CBGBs," Roger said. Pauling knew this was a nickname for the notorious Mexican drug cartel CJNG. That acronym stood for Jalisco New Generation Cartel, responsible for brutal murders on both sides of the border. "They've gone full throttle on their small-town approach. But even worse? They're finally taking on a big city. Guess which one?"

"Well, if you're working on it..."

"Yep," Roger admitted, without actually verbalizing it. "Hey, if you can make it on Broadway, you can make it anywhere."

Pauling knew what he was talking about, as well. Unlike most cartels who fought for major metropolitan areas like New York and Miami – the sites of some of the most brutal cartel turf wars of all time – CJNG focused on small communities where law enforcement was both local and minimal.

It was a strategy that had served them well as they'd expanded their empire and filled their coffers quite well over the past few years. Now, it sounded like they were going big-time.

"The many-headed hydra," Pauling said, referring to the sheer number of "soldiers" the cartels employed. It seemed whenever a kingpin was taken out, there were dozens more ready to take his (or sometimes her) place.

They ordered some appetizers and when those were done, as well as another round of drinks, people started to drop off.

Finally, it was just Pauling and Nicky.

"You know, this was more than just a social occasion," Nicky said. "Did you realize that or have you been out way too long?"

Pauling knitted her brows. "What are you talking about?"

"We could use you back at the Bureau. Osgood's retiring and there's been talk you'd be the perfect person to replace him."

"You've got to be kidding."

"What?" Nicky replied, counting off her points on her fingers. "One, you sold your company. Two, you're unemployed. Three, you're still single. What possible excuse could you have to not come back and work with me? We make a great team, you know that."

"Um, I don't have an excuse."

"Perfect. When can you start?"

Pauling laughed. She knew Nicky was only half-serious. "I said I don't have an *excuse*. But I have lots of good *reasons*." Now it was Pauling's turn to count off her points. "One, I don't need a paycheck. Two, my time at the Bureau was great, but I've moved on, permanently. And three, while I am still single, that doesn't mean I'm not in a relationship."

"Oh, is this the Tallon guy I've been hearing about?" Nicky said, her eyes wide with excitement. *Probably for the gossip*, Pauling thought.

"How did you know?" Pauling asked.

"Come on, Lauren. The FBI knows *everything*."

Pauling laughed. "Yes, Michael's a good guy. More importantly, we're really good together."

"When can I meet him?" Nicky actually rubbed her hands together which sent Pauling off into a fit of laughter.

When she was done, she realized Nicky was waiting for an answer.

"I don't actually know," Pauling replied.

CHAPTER EIGHT

The cheeseburger might be the greatest thing God had ever invented.

La Roca sat in the booth at the truck stop, some two hundred miles from his destination in Indiana, and looked at the culinary masterpiece before him. He thought of all the dry tortillas stuffed with bland beans he'd choked down in his lifetime. How it all seemed so incredibly poor in comparison to the beautiful concoction of bread (they called it a bun) meat, cheese, lettuce, tomato and onion. Not to mention the mayonnaise – another new word! – and pickles.

Next to the cheeseburger was a pile of yet another American brilliance: French fries. What kind of mad man could think up such a thing?

La Roca devoured his meal with great enthusiasm. He'd heard of people getting very fat eating American food; especially what they called "fast food." He didn't understand that term.

At the moment, he didn't care.

The food was absolutely delicious and getting fat seemed ridiculous. He was all muscle anyway. Besides, in his line of work, people didn't really worry about long-term health matters. Few lived long enough to experience them.

A truck driver sat down in the booth across from him. La Roca could feel the man's eyes upon him. He stayed focused on his food.

"Great, another Mexican," the man said.

La Roca looked up.

The man was staring at him. He had on a dirty baseball cap, greasy T-shirt. On his face was a scraggly red beard. A pale face and two bloodshot blue eyes stared back at him.

"You people are ruining this country," the trucker said.

La Roca focused on what was left of his cheeseburger.

A waitress came up to the truck driver's table. "Don't start nothin', Randall. We don't want no more trouble and if you cause a ruckus, Dale will kick you out of here once and for all."

She had glanced over at La Roca and smiled but he ignored her.

The waitress left and La Roca finished his meal. He put a twenty dollar bill on the table.

He sat and waited until the waitress brought the truck driver a plate of food. She cleared La Roca's plate and muttered a thank you for the tip.

When she left, he stood and walked to the truck driver's booth.

As he passed, he paused, placed a finger against one side of his nostril and blew out a gob of nasal mucous from the other nostril. It landed in the middle of the truck driver's hash browns.

The man gasped, dumbfounded, and La Roca walked to the men's room as he heard the truck driver scramble from the booth, cursing.

The waitress had turned her back on the dining area and was saying something to the cook who was busy flipping meat on a grill.

No one else seemed to notice.

La Roca walked into the men's room and waited. The door banged open and the truck driver stormed inside.

He didn't hesitate and immediately launched himself at La Roca.

The man's fist came around in a big looping swing and La Roca let it hit the side of his jaw.

His head bent under the blow, but he also heard bones in the man's hand break. La Roca's thick, powerful neck absorbed the force of the blow and the rest of his body showed no effect from the punch.

The truck driver howled with pain and La Roca waded in. He drove his massive skull forward and headbutted the man on the bridge of his nose. He heard the cartilage crunch under the force. The truck driver sagged. La Roca knocked the man's cap from his head, grabbed a handful of hair and smashed his face into the edge of the granite counter. The man's teeth sprinkled onto the bathroom floor like pennies dropped from someone's pocket. Blood gushed from the man's face and poured onto the bathroom floor.

La Roca smashed the man's face into the edge of the granite counter again. And again. And again.

The man's entire face was caved in and La Roca dropped him onto the floor. The truck driver's pants were sliding down and La Roca saw the top of his ass crack. He felt a stirring in his own pants.

When he'd been in prison in Mexico, he'd learned to appreciate the benefits of man-on-man sex. It had been some time since his last sampling, but he wondered if he should take the opportunity now. He thought he detected the man on the floor still breathing. That was good. He didn't want to have sex with a corpse.

But then the truck driver gave a last gasp and a spray of blood shot from the man's mouth. He gargled, and spasmed and then was still.

He was dead.

And so was La Roca's sexual desire.

For now.

He washed his hands at the sink and stepped over the dead truck driver.

He was only a few hours from Gideon, Indiana.

CHAPTER NINE

Tallon flew on a direct flight from New York to Las Vegas. He had an Uber driver take him out of Sin City all the way to his remote adobe ranch in the town of Independence Springs within a stone's throw of Death Valley.

He disabled the alarm system that cost the equivalent of a brand-new Porsche 911 (Turbo) and simultaneously unpacked and repacked. However, it was not an even exchange of gear.

His trip to New York to care for Pauling had been a civilian matter for the most part. Going to help Manny Ordonez find the people responsible for the murder of his friend's sister was most certainly not civilian in nature. The nice shirts, pants and shoes he'd taken to New York all went into the closet.

Out came the tactical gear: military-grade pants and shirts designed to hold various types of equipment. A wide variety of holsters for the selection of guns he would be bringing. Knives, ammunition, gloves, sunglasses, camouflage baseball cap and steel-toed boots.

For communication he would bring an industrial-grade laptop, a handful of burner cell phones and a satellite phone with encryption capabilities.

Next, he loaded provisions into his 4x4; a black Land Cruiser that weighed nearly the equivalent of a WWII battleship. In went bottled water, Gatorade and plenty of food that would last without refrigeration – trail mix, jerky and dried fruit.

Finally, Tallon unlocked the security doors to his weapons room. It was climate-controlled and the most heavily fortified room within a hundred miles. He studied the weapons before him and chose the best of each category he could envision needing. First, for close quarters he chose his favorite shotgun – a Mossberg Defender, 12 gauge. He'd already loaded a crate of double-aught buckshot that would knock Andre the Giant on his ass. For handguns, he chose his personal latest favorite, a Beretta .45 ACP with a high-capacity double-stack magazine that held 17 rounds. He had three of them and he packed two into a portable gun case, the third he slipped into a shoulder holster.

He added two more weapons under the premise it was better to have them and not need them, than to need them and not have them. Tallon added a HK (Heckler & Koch) MP5 submachine gun chambered in 9mm with a sound suppressor. Finally, his latest toy, a Russian-made Orsis T-5000 sniper rifle that fired the ridiculously powerful .338 Lapua Magnum. It was overkill, pun intended. Still, Tallon had been training with it for the past six months and he liked its ruggedness despite the high level of precision engineering. It was a rare combination in a rifle of this capability, and Tallon had come to admire the gun he referred to as his Russian girlfriend.

With his gear loaded, Tallon ate a quick meal, cleaned the kitchen, threw out any food that would go bad in his absence and sent a text message to Manny letting him know he would meet him at his place outside Indianapolis in a day and a half.

After two hours on the road, Manny still hadn't responded.

CHAPTER TEN

J uanita Navarro.
     Elizabeth Ordonez.
     Zoe Torres.
     Pitts studied the names and the corresponding files in the case folder she'd started when she'd been assigned the investigation. The IDs had come in and now, she looked the girls' information over; there wasn't much at all.

All three of them were from Mexico. They'd entered legally, all from the same region. It was the kind of information that had become quite common with the same issue; it was virtually impossible to confirm. While the paperwork from Mexico had no obvious reason to be doubted, it often was. The local police departments and government officials were often bribed by the criminals who held more power.

Often, American investigators like Pitts had no choice but to temporarily accept the data as valid. If fresh evidence told a different story, she would follow it wherever it led.

For now, she studied the files.

All of the dead women had been single. No children. No criminal past.

Pitts frowned.

What I'm looking at is a complete load of bullshit, she thought. Random crime was rare. Exceedingly rare. In fact, it was so rare that when it happened, most of the time books were written about the cases. Ninety-nine percent of the time a triple homicide like this did not come out of the blue. Pitts had a very strong feeling this was most certainly not the one percent portion of the equation.

Was it *possible*? Of course. These days, truth was often stranger than fiction. Yes, a lone wolf killer could have arbitrarily decided to kill these three women.

It was just all too neat.

Three women – and according to at least the initial people she'd spoken with – all of whom were quite pretty and attractive. Young. Single.

No kids. How often did that happen in and of itself? They were not sisters, their last names told that story. How often were three beautiful women, all in their mid-twenties, single with no children?

Not often.

Usually, at least one of them would have been married, or divorced, or had a kid. The fact that all three were exactly alike in that regard?

Red flag, Pitts thought.

And not the only one.

The other red flag? The three lovely, single, childless women jointly owned an auto repair shop and tire retail store. Again, not unheard of, but certainly out of the ordinary.

Pitts was all about female empowerment. As a black woman, she'd had to deal with both race and gender issues her entire career. Hell, she was only thirty-three years old and she felt like she'd fought a lifetime of that crap.

Still, how often did young women go into the auto repair and tire business?

Again, the percentages were against it.

Pitts sighed and drank the rest of her coffee. She was one of only three people in the local Gideon diner. The other two people were men whose combined age hovered around 160 years or so and judging by their flannel shirts, dirty jeans and work boots, most likely farmers. They had each sneaked surreptitious glances her way, probably marveling at seeing a black person in town. Even better – a woman! Big news!

Pitts closed the last of the files – this one on Elizabeth Ordonez – and slapped a ten-spot down on the counter. It was enough to cover her coffee and bagel along with a good tip. She figured she ought to treat the servers here right as she would likely be in town for a good amount of time.

She left the diner, got into her sedan and pointed it toward the apartment where the three girls had lived. Again – another anomaly – the three women lived together.

They co-owned a business yet didn't seem to mind living together. In other words, every waking moment was spent together. Didn't any of them have family? No need to get separate places to live? Most people who spent that much time together tended to get on each other's nerves; hence the need for separate living arrangements. But not these three. They worked together. Lived together.

And ultimately, died together.

Pitts thought it all seemed discordant, like a song sung slightly out of tune.

It took less than five minutes for her to find the apartment. It was a duplex. Probably built in the 70s. It had aluminum siding that had once been white and was now a muddled gray. The shingles on the roof were curling and Pitts noticed black granules at the ends of the downspouts. The grass was dead, the shrubbery thin and scraggly.

She parked the sedan and went up the front steps. Pitts knocked on the door but there was no response. She tried the front door. Locked. Around the back, she spied a carport where a beige, battered Nissan Altima was parked. She knew it was registered to Zoe Torres. The back door was locked.

Pitts checked her watch, went back to the sedan and found the landlord's name and phone number. She called and requested he come and unlock the apartment.

He would be there in twenty minutes. Pitts went to the other side of the duplex and noted the name above the mailbox.

Shurmur.

She pressed the doorbell. Inside, Pitts heard a television and then it was abruptly silenced. Footsteps on the floor and then the door opened a crack.

A man with a crewcut, flat nose and watery eyes peeked out at her.

"Yeah?" he asked.

She held up her badge. "Detective Pitts, Indiana State Police. Mind if I ask you a few questions about your neighbors next door?"

"Don't know nothing about those bitches," he said. "They never gave me the time of day. What, were they illegal immigrants? Don't surprise me one bit."

"Not exactly," Pitts said. "Did you ever see or hear anything unusual next door?"

"Nothing at all, like I said."

"Never had any issues with them?"

"Nope."

"What's your name?"

"Dick Shurmur. Why?"

Pitts jotted down the name in a notebook.

"I may have more questions for you later."

"Like I said, I don't know shit about them. They were uppity bitches, for sure. Believe that? Damn Mexicans acting all high and mighty."

His watery eyes narrowed.

"Why you askin' about 'em? If they ain't illegals, that is."

"They're dead. Someone murdered them."

The eyes widened.

"Holy shit," he said.

"Yeah."

A truck pulled up and Pitts turned. The man in the truck held up a set of keys. The landlord had arrived.

Pitts turned back to Shurmur.

"Well, thanks for chatting with me. If I have any more questions, and I probably will, I may stop back."

"Okay," he said. He glanced over as the landlord unlocked the door. "I can't believe someone killed them. You never know, do you?"

Pitts slid the notebook into her back pocket.

"No, sir. You never really do know."

CHAPTER ELEVEN

Tallon loved the open road. He remembered reading the book by Jack Kerouac when he was in his teens, how he'd loved the author's descriptions of the American countryside and the symbolism of one of the main character's lawlessness.

Of course, that had been years ago and now Tallon wasn't a young man anymore. He simply enjoyed the feeling of the miles rolling underneath him, the stretch of the highway ahead as it cut through mountain passes, the wheat fields and rolling hills, across rivers and into the country's heartland.

After fourteen hours on the road, he'd pulled into a cheap chain hotel, crashed on the bed, slept for six hours, and then took off again at dawn. By the time he reached the border of Indiana, it was nearly noon. He'd plugged in the address given to him by Manny and soon, he was cutting a swath through St. Louis, Illinois and rolling into Indiana on I-70. He veered north of Indianapolis until he reached a two-lane state highway and Tallon followed that until he entered a town called Elk Grove.

Tallon was not feeling good about the situation – Manny had not responded to any of his text messages or phone calls during the long drive.

There was a Holiday Inn that matched the address Manny had supplied. Tallon pulled the SUV into the lot, went into the hotel and took the stairs to Room 302. He knocked but there was no answer. He waited and sent yet another text that remained unanswered.

Tallon went back down to the lobby and approached the front desk.

"Can you do me a favor and call Manny Ordonez in Room 302?"

The hotel employee, a thin man with acne and the hint of a moustache, tapped the keys on a computer, nodded in agreement with Tallon's information and then picked up the phone. He pressed a single button and waited.

Tallon already knew there would be no answer.

"There's no answer," the man said. His name tag read "Troy."

"Okay, Troy," Tallon said. "Is there coffee over there?" He nodded his head toward a little serving bar that included a little glass display with some baked goods and bottled water.

"Yes sir."

"Okay, I'll just hang out a bit. Have you seen Mr. Ordonez lately?"

"No, but I just came on duty an hour ago."

Tallon walked over to the little hotel's counter and ordered a coffee from a Hispanic woman who was watching the television in the corner. Dr. Phil was talking to someone about personal limitations.

He took his coffee and sat at a table. There was virtually no activity. Dr. Phil droned on in the background behind him. An old man with a mop slowly made his way toward the restrooms at the back of the lobby.

Tallon spent a half hour waiting and checking the time on his Ball watch, then asked the coffee lady where the elevators were. She pointed toward a hallway to the left of the lobby.

Tallon walked down the hallway, past the

bathroom, to the stairwell, and took it to the third floor. He went quickly to Room 302, checking to make sure there were no security cameras at either end of the hall.

He took out a slim case with lock-picking tools and soon had the bolt slid back enough to push the door open.

Tallon slipped inside and shut the door behind him.

The room was empty. The bed was made. No luggage. No clothes in the closet. Tallon checked the bathroom. Empty. Unused.

He sat on the edge of the bed and checked his phone.

No messages.

Tallon looked around, smelled the typical hotel scent of carpet cleaner and deodorant used to mask the scents of thousands of people over dozens of years. Outside the window, the flat farmland of Indiana looked back at him. On the wall was an artsy black-and-white photo of a farm field showing rows of corn trailing off to a distant horizon.

Two things seemed fairly clear to Tallon.

One, Manny Ordonez was certainly not here.

And the second thought: he never had been.

CHAPTER TWELVE

The landlord's name was Taylor – Pitts wasn't sure if it was first or last and she wasn't going to bother finding out but then decided yes, it had to go in the case file so she clarified.

It was his first name. Taylor Wouts. He was beyond middle-aged, probably in his 60s and he wore khakis with a short-sleeved checkered shirt. It had a single pocket which held a pen and a notepad. He had a pot belly and said he was a retired schoolteacher and used the rentals as his only source of income.

He owned several apartment buildings in and around Gideon, most of them single family homes he'd converted to duplexes. But this was his only true duplex, originally designed to be a multi-family home. He'd rented the apartment to the three women nearly a year ago and he had no complaints about them as tenants.

"The only weird thing was they wanted to pay in cash, which was fine by me, but pretty unusual," he said.

Pitts studied the man more closely. His chest was slightly sunken in and he had dirty teeth that spoke of a lifelong smoker or tobacco chewer.

She saw the slight tenseness associated with fear and said to him, "Don't worry, I'm not with the IRS. I only want to find out who killed these women and as long as it doesn't involve your accounting practices, I don't care."

"Fair enough," the landlord said. He opened the front door for her and she stepped inside. He hesitated.

"Wait out here," she said. "You can lock up when I'm done."

"Yes, ma'am."

Pitts stepped inside the apartment and took a look around. There was a living room directly off the foyer. There was a worn couch with a colorful blanket, two recliners and a flat screen television sitting on top of a pine chest.

She walked in and saw a hallway that led to a kitchen. Off to the right was a staircase. Pitts went into the kitchen, noted the cleanliness and the smell of lemons.

There was a round table with three chairs, a fridge, stove and dishwasher. The floor was beige linoleum with a pattern that was mostly worn off, old but clean. Pitts opened some of the kitchen drawers but only found utensils and cooking implements. No notepads or phonebooks or accumulated mail.

Off the kitchen was a short hallway that convened in a small bathroom, also clean. The dining room held a long wooden table and six chairs. It looked like it had never been used and there was a thin film of dust on its surface.

She went up the stairs. Three bedrooms upstairs, no bathroom. Each room held a single bed, a dresser and a small closet. The clothes hanging in the closet were simple. A few shirts, slacks and the basics in terms of shoes.

There was nothing on the walls except for a single crucifix over each bed.

Pitts went back downstairs to the bathroom. She checked the medicine chest. Again, the bare necessities; toothpaste, toothbrushes, floss, some ibuprofen and antacid. No prescription medication. A single bottle of perfume. On the toilet tank was a box of Kleenex.

Back in the kitchen, Pitts opened the fridge. Milk. Cheese. Bread. A few plastic containers of leftovers. Lettuce. Fruit. Condiments.

She shut the door and went back to the foyer, checked around the front door for letters, or bills, even a newspaper.

There was nothing.

In addition to the lack of any mail, there were no computers. Not a single laptop, iPad or cell phone to be found anywhere. Not even chargers. Nothing personal. Not even medication with a person's name on it.

Were these women ghosts? Pitts wondered. No wonder they paid in cash – did they even have a checkbook?

Pitts jotted down the layout of the apartment, made some notes and then rejoined the landlord on the porch.

"Find anything?" he asked.

She ignored him and took out her phone.

Tapped an address into her map application.

It belonged to a business.

The Three Sisters Tire Company.

CHAPTER THIRTEEN

The decision seemed fairly simple; since Manny had summoned him here, Tallon would stay. At least for a day or two. Give his old brother-in-arms a chance to reappear, or at least let him know where he was.

So Tallon went back down to the lobby, booked a room a floor below Manny's empty room, and went out for dinner. He'd driven over twenty hours with only a short break. His plan was to eat dinner, go back to the hotel and get a good night's sleep. In the morning, he would figure out what to do.

There was a chain steakhouse a block from his hotel and he walked over to it. There was no wait so he went inside, ordered a beer and a T-Bone, and thought about the situation.

On impulse, he called Pauling.

"Hey," he said.

"How's it going?" she asked.

He filled her in on what he'd found.

"Has Manny ever done something like this before?"

"No."

Tallon watched as a group of men entered the steakhouse. They were all wearing golf attire and from their flushed faces, had spent a fair amount of time on the course knocking back alcoholic beverages.

"I've got a bad feeling something else is going on, something bigger than what he'd originally called me about."

"So what's the plan?"

"I was wondering if you could do me a favor," he said.

"Name it."

He used his phone to send Pauling Manny's contact information. "If you can, is there any way you can track Manny's phone? I know it's a lot to ask, but this is totally unlike him. And if he says something bad happened to his sister..."

"Of course," Pauling said. "I can probably get something to you by tomorrow morning."

"Thanks."

They talked a few minutes longer and he asked about how she was feeling. Stronger every day, was the reply.

They disconnected just as his steak appeared. He ate it slowly, skipping the potatoes and only partaking in the green beans as well. The meat was nothing special, but it hit the spot after the long drive. In the morning, he would use the hotel's little gym to get a workout in and then dive into whatever Pauling might have found.

If she had nothing for him, he would have to make a decision. Start investigating on his own or continue waiting. He would literally be starting from scratch, totally in the dark, if he decided to forge ahead without word from Manny. On the other hand, sitting in the Holiday Inn in Armpit, Indiana, wasn't a cause for excitement.

For now, the decision could wait until morning.

He didn't finish the steak or his beer, instead opting for a big glass of ice water. He paid his bill and strolled back to the hotel.

Along the way, he didn't notice the man in the blue suit, parked in a tan Crown Vic at the back of the parking lot. The man's eyes never left Tallon until he entered the hotel.

Then, the man picked up his cell phone and placed a call.

CHAPTER FOURTEEN

Pitts didn't see an auto repair shop and tire store marked The Three Sisters Tire Company.

Rather, she saw a giant red flag.

As in, the sight was just as strange as the apartment where the dead women had lived.

The shop was on the corner of a quiet intersection. Opposite was a craft store that looked empty. On the other side of the shop was a vacant lot and then an empty stretch before the first house appeared.

A car drove by occasionally.

The building itself was a perfect square, with a lower half made from painted cement block and the upper half beige aluminum siding. A wooden sign that had clearly been painted multiple times now had its current name in white letters with a red-and-black background.

It looked like the kind of business that made people wonder how it could possibly make enough money to survive. Then again, it was closed now and Pitts admitted that it could be a whole different story when it was open and business was good. Who knew? Maybe there was a ton of money in a little place like this. She kind of doubted it, but was determined to keep an open mind.

There were two main garage doors and a smaller office to the right. Maybe at some point there had been gas pumps but those were long gone now. Cracked concrete slabs stained with oil provided space for parking. There were overgrown weeds along the curb. Empty plastic bins that once held newspapers or community flyers now stood open. In one, someone had stuffed trash from a fast food restaurant.

The shop had been shut down, and she was sure the door to the office was locked. Pitts needed to track down the mechanic the women had hired to repair cars, but so far, she hadn't been able to find his name and contact information. Word was he actually lived in Chicago and only worked for the women part-time, when they had a project for him. Pitts would nail down those details in the next twenty-four hours.

For now, she wanted to see what exactly her three victims had been up to with their car repair business.

She walked around the perimeter of the building, noted the cars parked along one side. Pitts made a note to make sure each owner was contacted to find out if anyone was missing. Or were they vehicles yet to be repaired?

Behind the building, there was a dumpster and some scrap metal. Pitts peeked into the dumpster but it was empty save for rusty aluminum car trim.

Back at the front of the shop, she let herself in with the keys found in one of the dead women's pockets. Immediately, the smell of gasoline and tires overpowered her. She'd always secretly enjoyed the unusual smell of tires. At her Costco the tire section was next to the front doors and Pitts always stopped and savored the aroma.

Now, it didn't have the same effect.

She walked in and looked at the office. It was a single desk with a single chair.

How did that work, she wondered. *There were three of them.*

Pitts opened the desk drawer but saw nothing inside other than pens, paper clips, a pad of blank invoices and a dirty coffee cup.

There was no printer, copier or scanner. No phone, either.

A small fridge was tucked under the desk. She opened it and looked inside. Two bottles of Coca-Cola and a half-empty jar of salsa.

She shut the fridge doors, stepped from the office into the car bays via a doorway. The door was propped open and she took in the scene; it might have been the cleanest car repair shop she'd ever seen. The hoists were lowered so she couldn't see down inside the bays. A single work-bench spanned the entire rear of the garage with a few power tools and rags neatly organized at one end. A battered stool on wheels was tucked under the far side of the workbench.

Directly across from her was an air compressor and various hoists and cables attached to a network of metal arms extending from the ceiling. A vintage soda machine was next to the air compressor. Pitts walked over to it and studied it. She pressed one of the buttons but nothing happened. She found the power button on the air compressor and pushed it. Immediately, the compressor began to hum.

She turned it off.

Pitts made a tour of the entire garage, stopping to look at various stains on the floor and a calendar that was two months behind. It had a picture of Jesus on the current month and she noted it was from the Catholic church in Gideon.

Clearly, the crime scene techs had been here; there was fingerprint dust on the doors and in the office. She had little hope for a match, though.

Something was totally wrong with this picture.

These women hadn't been running an auto repair shop.

They hadn't even been living in that apartment. Oh, they'd technically stayed at the apartment, but it wasn't their home.

It was a temporary place to stay.

But why?

Her best guess: auto repair was not the real business enterprise at play here.

So what business had the three women really been conducting?

CHAPTER FIFTEEN

The craft store wasn't empty.

It had definitely gone out of business, but there was one occupant watching Detective Pitts work her way through the car repair shop.

La Roca was watching from the second floor of the abandoned business. He'd parked his car two blocks away, broken the flimsy lock on the back door of the place, and climbed the stairs to the second floor. He'd even found a ratty wicker rocking chair in a different room and had dragged it over by the window so he could watch the repair shop and wait for the right moment.

Not yet.

It wasn't dark.

Besides, he had watched the black lady cop poke around inside. She'd left fifteen minutes ago but he had no idea if she would come right back. Maybe she'd taken a quick look and would be back in a little bit with a partner, or a bigger squad.

La Roca didn't know so he kept doing what he'd been trained to do: wait.

What he'd seen of this little town amused him. So neat and clean. He knew that in America it was a place not considered fancy. It was probably thought of as what he'd heard they call "middle class."

Whatever the hell that meant.

Compared to the little village he'd grown up in back in Mexico, this place was like heaven. No roving gangs of thugs ready to murder, rape and torture innocent people. (He didn't include himself in that class of people even though most would.) From what he'd seen in Gideon, garbage didn't litter the streets, children weren't sleeping on sidewalks with rags for clothes and rats didn't outnumber the humans.

No, as far as he was concerned, Gideon, Indiana, was a fine place.

His superiors had clearly thought so.

La Roca watched and waited. A boy riding a bicycle went through the intersection. He was talking on his phone as he rode his bike. The boy reminded him so much of this country. A, what do you call that word – a symbol. La Roca nodded to himself in the growing darkness as the sun sunk below the horizon.

The boy was a symbol of America; careless, oblivious, with a false sense of security. In Mexico, especially in his village, no one felt safe. Therefore, they were always careful. They took guns everywhere. They rarely traveled alone. And if there was a threat, they neutralized it before it could materialize.

La Roca had killed his first man before he was even ten years old. An old drunk in the village who'd tried to force him to take off his pants. As a boy, he'd always carried a small knife and he remembered how he had stabbed the old man in the chest over and over, feeling the warm blood gush out onto his hand.

It had been the most thrilling moment of his life.

When he went to the place he called home – both of his parents were dead – he was a hero for defending himself. They gave him tequila and called him a man.

How different than the boy on the bike below.

Finally, the setting sun was gone and the street below was filled with shadows. Even the sparse traffic had drained down to nothing. A car hadn't passed through in the last ten minutes.

La Roca figured the woman detective would not be coming back today. Why would she wait for darkness to fall and then come back? If she had a partner or the people who tested for finger-prints and fibers and all that stuff they show on the television, she certainly would have preferred to do it during the day.

Now was as good a time as any.

La Roca slipped out of the wicker rocking chair, went down the stairs, outside and crossed the street. He strolled past the repair shop, then detoured into the alley behind the shop, by the dumpster. It was pitch-black here.

He used a switchblade knife to jimmy the back door and then he was inside.

Something scurried in the dark behind him but he knew it was a mouse or something similar. There was just the faintest bit of light coming in from the office area. Either a clock with a bright display, or maybe an answering machine. Some-thing small.

La Roca turned to his right and walked the

length of the shop, the long rectangular work-bench guiding him. When he reached the end, he turned and stopped. In his early years when he'd done as much burglary as killing, he'd often felt a sense of calm and peacefulness in the dark. Now was no exception. How long he waited, he wasn't sure.

But when it felt right, he moved silently up to the vintage soda machine. He traced its side with his hands. He steadied his feet, tightened his grip on the edges of the machine, and pulled. He was powerfully built, but he used a controlled motion. The big machine hesitated, then surrendered to his efforts.

It slid forward.

La Roca pulled until he figured he had opened up at least four feet of space behind the machine. He went around behind it, and knelt down. Reached out and felt for the object he was looking for.

And then he felt it.

The dial.

He withdrew a penlight from his pocket and used his bulk to shield the light. Most of it would be blocked by the vending machine, but he was always a careful man.

He turned the dial so it matched the numbers

in his head and then he stopped, found the latch and pulled the safe door open.

The penlight swept up and illuminated what lay inside.

"Dios mio," La Roca said.

CHAPTER SIXTEEN

The little hotel gym provided just enough equipment to let Tallon enjoy a good workout. He was getting older, no doubt about it. He looked at himself in the mirror; over six feet, narrow hips, broad shoulders, arms roped with muscle. His face was that of a fighter; a man born for battle. No one would ever accuse him of being "Hollywood" yet at the same time, he had never had difficulty attracting women.

It was interesting to see how he struggled to lift the same amount of weights but with much greater difficulty than even ten years ago. The bench press, concentration curls, lat pulldowns. It all seemed harder. But he refused to give in and lower his weight totals.

Not yet.

Maybe one day.

Pauling was trying to convince him to start approaching fitness in a different way. More body-weight exercises, flexibility, breathing. He was skeptical but at the same time knew at some point he would have to agree with her.

He just wasn't ready quite yet.

Now, he showered, dressed, checked his phone and laptop for messages. There were none.

Downstairs in the hotel's dining area, he had a light breakfast of oatmeal, fruit and coffee.

With his laptop open on the table next to his plate, he double-checked his email but saw no messages from anyone.

Tallon sipped his coffee and thought about Manny Ordonez. What details could he remember about him that might help him begin the investigation on his own? He seemed to remember Manny had been born in Texas, grew up in New Mexico and joined the military right out of high school.

If Tallon remembered correctly, he hadn't been from a big family. Was the sister Manny claimed had been killed his only sibling? For some reason, Tallon thought so, but he couldn't be sure.

He logged into a private military database for

which he paid a monthly fee. The access was ostensibly provided for networking opportunities, but it was also possible to perform limited research on individuals. Tallon had used it a time or two mostly to check out other members of a proposed mission. In each case, they had checked out as legitimate.

Now, he typed in the extent of information he had about Manny Ordonez. It wasn't a lot. Name, branch of military, approximate age and birthplace. Tallon waited for the computer to process his request. A family came into the breakfast area and Tallon smiled at the harried Mom. She looked like she'd been up all night.

When he glanced back down at his screen, there were no fewer than a dozen matching records. He sped through them, discarding files for "other" Manny Ordonezes. With that done, he had less than five files, all of them regarding his friend. They were boilerplate, unfortunately. Name, rank, logistical records and promotions.

Only one thing caught Tallon's eye; at one point, Manny had listed a home address in Chicago. That was a surprise. He'd never heard his friend mention the Windy City. Tallon jotted down the address. As he did so, his phone rang.

It was Pauling.

"Hey," he said.

"I struck out on your friend's cell phone," she said. "It's had no activity since the day he contacted you and according to the phone company's record, it last pinged on a tower about a half-mile from where you're staying."

Tallon frowned. That was bad news.

"And then I have some more bad news," she said. "Or worse news, I guess."

"About his sister?"

"Yeah, I was able to find his family's records. His parents are both deceased, but he had one sibling, a sister. Her name was Elizabeth Ordonez."

"Elizabeth," Tallon said. "Yeah, I remember he mentioned the name Liz a time or two."

"Unfortunately, she's dead. She was murdered in a little town north of you called Gideon. The Indiana State Police are investigating. A detective named Pitts is in charge."

Tallon closed his laptop and finished off his coffee.

"Okay, that's where I'm going, then," he said.

"Be careful," Pauling answered. "I'll forward you the information I have but it was a multiple homicide. Three women hung from a highway overpass."

"Understood, and thanks," Tallon said.

He gathered his gear and went out to his vehicle.

A triple homicide, he thought. And if Manny was dead, that made it four.

Tallon was beginning to get angry but he also had no illusions. If someone was able to take out Manny – who would have been on high alert, probably armed and ready for battle – this wasn't an amateur at work.

A grim expression crossed his face. Not a smile.

Good, he thought. *It'll make killing the person or people responsible all the more rewarding.*

CHAPTER SEVENTEEN

"He said his name was Reacher?"

Roquelle rolled her eyes at the cop. "Didn't I just say that?"

They were in the doorway of a tiny apartment in the bad part of town. Which was sad because out here on Long Island, the villages were barely big enough to even have a bad section. Roquelle shared the place with her mom. That's how she thought of it: sharing. Most kids say they live with their parents but Roquelle shared the expense of paying for the apartment. If anything, she was letting her mom live here, not the other way around.

As usual, Roquelle's mother was nowhere to be found, probably off at the bar getting drunk with her latest "friend."

The cop, a middle-aged white guy with thick glasses sighed, then stopped writing in his little notebook. He peered at her through his lenses, making him look like a googly-eyed lizard.

"Reacher? Is that his first name or last?"

"How would I know? I barely met the guy."

Roquelle giggled.

"You don't seem to understand," the cop said. "I just informed you your friend Tanya was found murdered in a motel room a half-mile from here. According to her friends, the last thing she told them was that she was going on a double date with you."

"Yeah that's not true but even if it was, so what?"

"So if you had anything to do with it, or if you don't cooperate, you could be considered an accessory to murder. Is the possibility of spending your life in prison something you want to laugh about?"

"Give me a freakin' break," she said. "It wasn't a double date. Tanya said she wanted to make some money and we knew a guy who liked young girls. She needed a ride out there is all."

"That's the complete opposite of what Tanya's friends say. They say you knew the guy and you were calling the shot."

"Nope. Tanya told me he booked her a hotel room and arranged to meet him. She just needed a ride so I borrowed my mom's car and dropped her off there, that's all I know."

Not really, she thought to herself. *I know a lot more but I'm sure as hell not telling.*

"You left her alone with some guy the two of you hardly knew?"

"Like I said, I was just doing her a favor. How was I supposed to know he was going to kill her?"

The detective looked exasperated, like he wanted to slap her. Instead, he wrote something down in his notebook.

"How did you communicate with this Reacher fella?"

"Cell phone." She whipped out her phone and showed the cop the number the man had given her and Tanya. The cop jotted that down, too.

"I want you to stay in town for the next few days," he said. "I may need you to come into the station and make a statement. In fact, I know I will. Maybe when your mom comes home you can call me. Do you have a car?"

"Nope, not at the moment. If my mom meets a guy at the bar, I don't have one tomorrow, either."

"Okay, I can send someone to bring you in. If

you hear of anything, or if this Reacher guy calls you again, call me right away."

He handed her a business card which she knew she would throw into the trash as soon as he left.

"You got it," she said. The sarcasm was there, but if the detective noticed, he let it slide.

He left and Roquelle shut the door. She grabbed her phone, tapped the number she'd just shown to the cop and put the phone to her ear.

"The cops were just here because Tanya is dead, you bastard." Her voice had risen to a shrill scream. "Bastard!"

She hung up and tried not to burst into tears.

CHAPTER EIGHTEEN

The man who had called himself Reacher – it wasn't his real name – listened to Roquelle make her phone call. He didn't answer, of course. The burner cell phone he'd used to arrange the rendezvous with the girls was long gone, destroyed and broken into a dozen pieces dumped by the side of a road in the middle of nowhere.

But due to his position in life, and his professional occupation, he'd been able to place surveillance of the highest priority on Roquelle's phone and he now knew the cops had discovered poor Tanya's beautiful body.

His manhood stirred at the memory of that exquisite specimen. He'd enjoyed her every which way and then let his darkest desire take over. Killing her had not been his objective, but in the frenzied throes of his flammable passion he'd done the deed and choked the very life out of her.

Oh, he'd known the cops would find Tanya.

He'd also known they would question Roquelle.

Mostly, he'd been curious how she would react. The girl was street-tough and hated cops so he figured she would stonewall them out of sheer spite.

He knew he was right because at the moment he was looking at the detective's case notes – another surveillance order that had been placed without question.

The man who called himself Reacher leaned back and looked out his window.

It was possible he had too many irons in the fire, he had to admit. He was playing a game with very high stakes and this thing with the girls was just a side hustle. The other stuff was important because a mistake in that regard would ensure him a horrible outcome and he was determined to be ahead of the curve.

Maybe he should have waited until the stuff in Indiana was settled, but young female flesh was for him the ultimate source of pleasure and stress release.

It was so nice to work in law enforcement at the highest levels.

It was like having keys to the candy store.

CHAPTER NINETEEN

P itts let out a low, long whistle.

The results were back from the license plates recorded at Three Sisters Tire Company. The results had been cross-referenced to identify any of the vehicle's owners with criminal background, specifically violent crime.

One name had been a match.

Wayne Adams.

Burglary. Disorderly conduct. Numerous traffic violations. A weapons charge.

Pitts noted the man's address and plugged it into her GPS. The route took her out of Gideon into cornfields and the occasional clapboard home in need of paint. The air smelled vaguely of cow manure and fresh hay.

The sun was still low in the sky – it was late

morning and Pitts hadn't slept well in the cheap hotel on the outskirts of town. The bed had been saggy and she hadn't trusted the cleanliness of the room. She couldn't wait to see this case through and get back home.

Eventually, she reached a mailbox upon which numbers had been applied using cut pieces of black electrical tape. She pulled her car into the driveway, parked and approached the house.

From the backyard, a dog began to bark. She stepped up onto the porch, noted the peeling paint, loose floorboards and overgrown weeds that were now shooting up through the wood slats in the floor.

Pitts knocked on the front door and a few pieces of paint flittered into the air, looking like beige-colored snowflakes caught in the sun.

There was a loud bang inside and then the door was jerked open.

"Yeah?"

It was a woman with missing front teeth, a T-shirt that read *You are my sunshine*, dirty jeans and a barefoot.

"What the hell?" the woman asked.

"I'm looking for Wayne Adams, is he around?"

"Shit, you know what's best for you, you

oughta turn around and drive on out of here," the woman said. "Wayne don't care for your kind."

Pitts took out her badge and flashed it before the woman's eyes.

"Have him come out and talk to me," she said. "Or I can come back with a warrant, a dozen officers and we'll arrest every barefooted cracker we see."

The woman's face flushed a bright red and she slammed the door shut. Pitts adjusted her stance so she had ready access to the pistol on her hip.

Eventually, the door opened and a little man who looked like a cross between a librarian and a garden gnome peered up at her.

"What does your black ass want?" he asked.

"We're investigating the murders of three women and I wanted to talk to you about your connection with them," Pitts said. She kept her voice even and it took great effort. "Apparently, you brought your car to their repair shop?"

"So?"

"Well, did you know the three women who ran the shop?"

"Them three Mexes? Hell no. I left it with their mechanic, Jimmy. He's a good ol' boy, did all the work for them – ran the place practically. Heard someone strung them up." His eyes narrowed and he said to her, "Nice to have a lynching around here again. Like the good old days."

Pitts cocked her head to one side. She could just shoot him, claim he resisted arrest. The thought was nice, but she knew she wouldn't.

"They were killed two nights ago," Pitts said. "Where were you?"

"I was at a meetin' over in Sawbrush. At least a dozen people saw me there. No way I could've been back here in Gideon."

"What was the meeting?"

He cackled. "Oh, wouldn't you like to know?"

"Don't tell her, Wayne!" the woman inside the house called out.

The old man leaned down and whispered conspiratorially, "Ever hear of the Viele Waffen?"

"Can't say I have."

"Look it up and don't come back!"

He stepped back and slammed the door shut.

CHAPTER TWENTY

As Tallon drove, the anger didn't dissipate. It merely morphed, very slowly, into something harder, darker and more resolute.

He'd quickly skimmed the information Pauling had sent him about the three murdered women in Gideon, wanting to understand the gist of it before he got behind the wheel.

There was no doubt in his mind that he would continue pursuing the truth behind what was going on. Yes, it felt a bit strange to him to be driving to a small town in Indiana he knew nothing about to possibly investigate the murder of a woman he had never met.

Yet, the bond between men like himself and Manny was beyond strong. It was more than duty.

More than friendship. Something that was a combination of the two but much stronger and lasting.

Besides, he knew that Manny would have done the same thing for him.

So he gunned the big Land Cruiser on toward Gideon. There was very little traffic and he found himself unconsciously looking for the cell phone tower that may have signaled the last time his friend had been by. He saw no towers and within two hours was approaching town.

He was driving a little over the speed limit and came up behind a sedan that screamed police to him. It was big and heavy, with a beefed-up suspension and an extra aerial on the roof.

Tallon was close enough to see that a black woman was behind the wheel; another oddity as he'd seen very few African Americans since his arrival in rural Indiana.

She had to be a cop. And not just a regular officer. No, she would probably be a detective. What had Pauling said? The Indiana State Police were investigating. So she was a homicide detective from ISP.

A big gun.

At first he thought it was weird luck that he

just happened to pull up behind her but then he wondered if it was more than just a coincidence.

According to Pauling's messages, it had been a triple homicide. That kind of thing out here would get a lot of attention. How many African American detectives lived in Gideon, Indiana? The town was so small that until the case was solved, there would be plenty of cops around and if he stayed, he was bound to run into them, sooner or later.

He decided to drop back a little bit and follow her into town.

She drove ahead and soon they were entering the little community, underneath the very overpass that said "Welcome to Gideon" that Tallon figured was the original crime scene.

He drove on and spotted the black cop as she parked outside a diner.

Tallon drove past her and watched as she exited the car and went inside. There was a whole row of empty parking spots along Main Street so Tallon pulled into the nearest one, parked and went into the diner and spotted the cop sitting at the back. She had her phone out and a thick binder with a notepad and a pen. She glanced up at him, looked down, then back up.

He strolled past the counter and a glass case

full of homemade pies. The apple looked especially tempting. A waitress said, "Sit anywhere,
hun."

Tallon walked up to the booth. The black cop
was looking at him.

"Mind if I join you, Detective?" he asked.

"Do I know you?"

"No, but I think we have a mutual interest.
Elizabeth Ordonez. One of the murdered
women."

"What about her?"

"Her brother asked me to help him look into
who killed her."

"So that's your business, not mine."

Tallon slid into the booth and waited as the
waitress appeared and put a glass of water in front
of him. He asked for a cup of coffee and a slice of
apple pie.

After the waitress left, Tallon turned his
attention back to the detective.

"My friend, the one who asked me to help
him?"

"Yeah?"

"Well, he's missing."

CHAPTER TWENTY-ONE

One of things he loved about his big Buick, a beautiful American car, was its enormous trunk.

It was really hard to believe, La Roca mused. A vehicle that rode so comfortably also had so much space in the back. It was incredible, really. Everything in America was bigger and better. Vehicles like this in Mexico would be cobbled together with spare parts and would bounce all over the road, the engine would be loud and you couldn't drive into the desert for fear you'd never make it back.

Now, he'd pulled the Buick into the alley behind the repair shop and loaded the items from the safe behind the vintage soda machine into the trunk.

There were approximately twenty wrapped packages, a mix of sizes, sealed in plastic wrap. Having worked in the business for some time, La Roca knew the packages contained a mixture of heroin, cocaine, methamphetamine and opioids.

There was one item, though, that he hadn't been expecting.

He'd known there would be a cache of drugs. And loads of cash. There were always those two things surrounding everything in his business.

But this thing?

He hadn't been expecting it.

When the safe door had swung open, and he'd seen the cavernous space inside, he wasn't surprised. It could have been a safe room, too. Big enough for at least half a dozen people to hide inside.

But there were no people inside.

At least not alive.

A dead man sat strapped into a chair. He'd been beaten pretty thoroughly. His face was misshapen and his clothes were covered in blood.

La Roca patted the man's bloody shirt and felt in the pants pockets. He came out with a wallet and a New Mexico driver's license.

Manny Ordonez it read.

La Roca tossed the wallet and license onto the

floor. Whatever happened to the dead man was not his concern. He had his orders and he intended to follow them. The dead man was a mystery he had no desire to solve.

He walked back through the garage, out to the Buick and drove away.

It was as simple as that. No shootout, no rival gang ready to ambush him. America was the land of plenty, someone had said. He saw no point in disagreeing.

Hours later, when he checked into a chain hotel far from Gideon in a whole different state, he used one of the disposable mobile phones stashed in the car's glove compartment.

He rang a number and waited until someone answered.

"I need to speak to Jefe," he said.

CHAPTER TWENTY-TWO

Pitts looked across the table at the man who seemed to have no small amount of confidence. He'd said his name was Michael Tallon.

Not a bad-looking guy, not at all, she thought. A little rough around the edges maybe, but cleaned up he'd do just fine.

Not that she was in the market.

Her divorce was over two years ago and she'd been dating ever since. She was still in an on-again/off-again relationship with the principal of an elementary school. He was a good man, but most of the time her job caused issues. She carried a gun, after all. Chased down bad guys. Sometimes she had to kick some ass. A lot of guys were intimidated by that and often felt the need to overcompensate by being complete assholes.

So far, the educator was okay, but her intuition had started to kick in; she could see storm clouds on the horizon.

"So your friend asked you to come help find out who killed his sister? And now he's missing?" she asked.

"That's right," Tallon said.

"How long?"

"Oh, you're going to give me the twenty-four-hour business?"

"No, because you're not family, am I right? I don't even need to rely on that."

Tallon sipped his coffee. They were talking about how law enforcement usually required a twenty-four hour time period or longer before they would actively begin a missing persons investigation. A good rule as all too often the missing person would return home on their own accord, surprised by all the drama that had transpired since they'd gone off on some perfectly innocent sojourn.

"You're not family," Pitts said. "He's been missing for less than twenty-four hours and I've got a triple homicide I'm working on."

"That is most likely related."

"You don't know that."

Pitts had her laptop open and had sent an email to her chief back at ISP. She'd quickly typed up the latest and sent it to him, including a request for more information on the Viele Waffen.

"What I do know is that we're both here for the same thing," Tallon said.

Pitts rolled her eyes. "There you go with your assumptions. You don't know what I'm working on and let's be honest, law enforcement professionals don't generally mix with civilians, so I suggest you move along. Your claims that Manny Ordonez is missing have been duly noted."

The waitress brought a slice of pie and Pitts wished she'd ordered some herself.

"Mind if I finish my pie?" he asked her. He was smiling a little bit and she almost laughed, too. But she held it in check.

"You know what? Let me try a taste of that." She used a fork to break off a chunk of pie. My Lord it was good.

"So sharing is okay when it comes to dessert," Tallon said.

Pitts smiled this time. She liked this Michael Tallon.

"As long as it doesn't involve my case, we can share all sorts of things."

Tallon's face turned just the slightest tinge of pink and Pitts felt a deep sense of satisfaction. It wasn't often she could make a good-looking man like Michael Tallon blush.

Hell, she enjoyed that more than the pie.

CHAPTER TWENTY-THREE

Tallon was amused by Detective Pitts. She was sharp, and her dark eyes always seemed to be filled with a skeptical humor, as if she was secretly enjoying whatever he'd been saying to her.

He'd left the diner without much to show for the encounter. Pitts had given him very little information, although he believed in a pinch she would be willing to help him if it meant success for her in this case.

Tallon looked up and down the main street of Gideon. Not much to see, really. He considered driving down to the local police station but figured he'd get an even colder reception than the one Pitts had offered.

He walked back to his SUV, got inside and

started it up. His laptop was in a backpack in the passenger side foot space and he dug it out, connected to the internet via a hotspot he'd set up on his phone, and read the articles Pauling had forwarded to him regarding the triple homicide.

In one of the articles, it mentioned the Three Sisters Tire Company, as well as the address, sans the street number, of the apartment where the victims had lived.

It wouldn't be a problem to figure that one out. Tallon used the map on his phone to find the street and then he put the Land Cruiser in gear and drove. He was reminded of how nice it would be to live in a small town; you could go from one side of town to the other in a few minutes.

He passed quiet streets where no one was out and about. An old church with a beautiful steeple was the most impressive structure in town, but that too was empty at this time of day.

Tallon turned onto the street and drove slowly looking for the house. He spotted the police tape on a duplex and knew that was the spot. Driving past, he reached the end of the street and pulled to the curb.

A duplex was bad. A shared wall, no doubt. If the people on the other half were home, it was quite possible he'd be discovered if he tried to slip into the apartment where the victims had lived. Plus, while the street was quiet, who knew if there was a little old lady sitting in her living room crocheting a scarf for a grandchild while steadfastly scrutinizing any and all activity near her house?

No, he wouldn't be going into that apartment now.

Only as a last resort.

Instead, he would focus on the business. The address was easy to find, as was the repair shop. It was on a corner in a commercial section of town. Across the street was an abandoned craft store. The perfect place if he wanted to set up shop and do some surveillance.

That wouldn't be necessary.

He had, after all, just made a long drive in the vehicle. Maybe he heard something on the trip? Like a ticking sound in the suspension and he wanted a mechanic to take a look. A perfectly justified reason to pull into the shop and go knocking on the doors.

Tallon pulled the SUV right into the Three Sisters Tire Company driveway and parked. He went with brazen confidence to the front door and knocked loudly. There was no answer and the door was locked.

He peered inside but the windows were dirty and the shop was dark.

Tallon walked around the building to the back door.

It was ajar.

He stepped inside and drew his Beretta .45 ACP from his shoulder holster and waited. There wasn't a sound inside. His eyes slowly adjusted to the dark interior and he took note of the long workbench that ran the length of the shop. Tallon could smell oil and grease tinged with the faint scent of cigarette smoke.

There was another odor, too. Something that had no substitute.

Death.

With his vision fully adjusted, Tallon immediately spotted the vintage soda machine at the other end of the shop. It was pulled away from the wall.

Careful to make no sound, he walked slowly along the length of the workbench until he could see behind the machine. It was a huge safe with a nearly floor-to-ceiling door. Inside, there was a dead man strapped to a chair. With the Beretta out in front of him, Tallon stepped inside the space. The room was empty, save for the lone occupant.

The dead man appeared to be of Hispanic descent. He'd clearly been beaten and tortured. A wallet was on the floor, open to the driver's license. Tallon holstered his gun and used a small flashlight to illuminate the name on the license, even though he was already certain he'd found his friend.

"Ah, shit," Tallon said.

CHAPTER TWENTY-FOUR

The tiny Gideon Police Department consisted of one Chief of Police – a man named Tomkins, and the young officer Pitts had already met, whom she'd dubbed "Farm boy."

They'd given her a desk and a computer with a printer if she needed it and after she'd left the café and begun to research the Viele Waffen, Pitts had opted to go into the office and work. It would just be faster and easier to get things done there.

The department was a poorly constructed aluminum shed outfitted with office equipment. There were no more than five rooms in total and the place smelled like a hardware store. Pitts sat at her desk and read with great interest what she'd learned so far about the group Wayne Adams had used for his alibi.

The first thing she learned was that Viele Waffen loosely translated in English to "Many Weapons." It was clearly a white supremacist group and although there wasn't a lot about them on the Internet and on ISP's collected files, there was enough to tell her they believed in a decentralized effort. Meaning small, isolated "cells" that acted independently for the most part.

Which made her wonder why Wayne Adams had claimed there was a meeting of at least "twenty or so" people, as he'd put it. It sounded like that kind of meeting went against their organizational philosophy. If so, why had they held it? Perhaps a triple homicide?

Pitts worked for another hour and then did a conference call with her boss back at ISP. Help was on the way, she was told. Two more detectives were coming to help chase down leads and follow up on witness statements. They would have been there sooner but had just finished nailing a meth ring down near Corydon, Indiana.

That was fine with Pitts. Her partner of ten years had just left the force and moved to California to become a wine journalist, which sounded like a load of bull to Pitts. Instead of drinking on the job, it sounded like drinking *was* the job.

"So you think this was a hate crime?" her superior asked her. "These white power Waffen guys? Killed three innocent Hispanic women?"

"Maybe," Pitts said. "I think there's more to it, though."

"Like what?"

"It's still early, but something's wrong with this, Chief. The apartment where the victims lived? It looked like temporary digs. Nothing permanent, no mail, no signs of an actual permanent life being created."

"So they were minimalists," her boss countered. "Isn't there some Japanese lady talking about decluttering? A bestselling book and a television show about living simply?"

"Wow, listen to you," Pitts said. "Up on your popular culture, I like that."

"But you're not feeling that?"

"No, I'm not. The business was strange, too. It looks like they'd hired a mechanic to do the actual repair work, but then the three of them ran the office. The problem is – I looked at the office and it doesn't look like much was being done. At all. As in, virtually nothing."

There was silence on the line.

"Then what were they doing?"

Pitts waited a moment, then gave him her best guess.

"You remember that drug ring we busted down by Terra Haute? Linked to a cartel?"

"Yeah, what about it?"

"Remember we flipped one of their guys and he said the big push from their bosses over the order was to focus on small towns?"

"Oh yeah, they had a really weird name, right?" her boss said. "Something New Kids?"

Pitts almost laughed. "Jesus, New Kids on the Block? No, that's not what they were called."

"Okay, then what?"

"Jalisco New Generation," Pitts said. "Or maybe you remember their abbreviation: CJNG."

CHAPTER TWENTY-FIVE

"I t was all there?"

El Jefe didn't mince words with his top Sicario. "Sicario" was the Spanish word for hitman, and La Roca was known as the most dangerous in the country. His name instilled fear and El Jefe liked to wield his weapon whenever he could.

"Yes." La Roca repeated the extent of what he'd found, including the dead man. He was standing in the parking lot, using a burner cell phone, far from the crimes in Gideon. This call would be untraceable and he would destroy the phone immediately afterward. Nonetheless, they spoke in code words just in case the conversation was being recorded.

"The last part is disappointing," El Jefe said,

referring to La Roca's report of the dead man who'd been tortured and killed.

La Roca could picture his boss in his mind. He was lean and strong, with a long neck and a beak of a nose. Sometimes, La Roca thought of him less as El Jefe and more like El Giraffe.

"It seems our friend in New York has forgotten who he is dealing with," El Jefe said. "I want you to go there and remind him."

La Roca had never met the man, but El Jefe had provided him with a name, a photo and an address. It was all he needed.

"Do you want him to survive the encounter?" La Roca clarified.

"It's a lesson I want him to take to the grave."

CHAPTER TWENTY-SIX

"Shit," Pitts said.

"That's what I said."

Tallon had called the ISP Detective and told her what he'd found at the repair shop. He'd stuck with a flimsy cover story: It had been unlocked and he'd just wanted to get some work done on his SUV before he drove back to California.

He knew she wouldn't buy it, but he needed her there.

His friend was dead, he'd been brutally murdered and now he wanted revenge. But he didn't want to be arrested for not reporting a crime and besides, he liked Pitts. His gut instinct said to trust her.

Within minutes, she had arrived on the scene.

"Thanks for calling me."

"Yeah, I kind of had to. We should call this in," Tallon said as they both studied the body of Manny Ordonez.

Pitts didn't respond.

She was studying the safe room.

"Shit, I can't believe my guys missed this. Our CSI guys are really good."

"No reason for them to look for a safe. It wasn't the scene of the crime, either," Tallon pointed out.

"I should have been smarter," Pitts said. "I knew this business was some kind of front, I just hadn't had time to prove it."

"What were they running? Drugs? Weapons? Both?" Tallon asked.

Pitts sighed. "I trust you enough to tell you they were probably linked to a group in Mexico who's known for branching out to small towns to distribute their product. We already ran up against them in southern Indiana. It wouldn't surprise me if they were working their way north."

"Less scrutiny in small towns."

"Yeah."

Tallon thought about his friend Manny. Had he known his sister was involved with a drug operation? One that was possibly linked to a Mexican cartel? Maybe, maybe not. Either way, he couldn't ask him now.

Off to their right, they both heard a car door close.

"Did you call for backup?" Tallon asked.

"Backup?" Pitts scoffed. "Hell, in this town there is no backup."

And then the room exploded in gunfire.

CHAPTER TWENTY-SEVEN

Pitts was knocked off her feet and Tallon threw himself away from the sound of the shots. He landed on the concrete floor and was partially covering her body as glass from the garage doors rained down on them. Tallon had his Beretta in his hand and dragged Pitts behind a rolling metal toolbox. It wouldn't provide much cover, but it was better than nothing.

He saw a group of silhouettes outside the garage doors and did not like the number. At least a dozen of them. Off to his left, another pair of shadows were peering in from the office.

These he could partially make out because they had fired through the office door and one of them was now peering through it. It was a white man's face with a beard and a baseball cap.

Tallon fired instinctively without aiming, and the man's head exploded in a shower of blood and brain matter. The Beretta fired a .45 ACP and he'd loaded the high-capacity magazine with hollow points. It was a self-defense round. Not the fastest bullet in the world, but when it arrived it packed a wallop and the bullet fragmented, causing enormous damage.

The second shadow in the office ducked for cover and Tallon fired but knew he missed. The shooters outside the garage doors were inching closer and Tallon was angered by their arrogance. They weren't even taking cover, as if the sheer number of them would protect them from return fire.

Well, he was about to change that.

He brought the Beretta up and started on his left, firing as if he were shooting along a line of targets, which technically, he was.

He shot from sheer muscle memory, his finger working the trigger, the front sight more in his mind's eye than in focus as his eyes followed the line of shooters who'd just ambushed he and Pitts.

Tallon had no way of knowing if his shots found their targets as he shot with a fluid motion, under control but with no wasted energy. When his slide locked back, he shucked the empty magazine and rammed the new one home.

Beneath him, Pitts stirred. She was kneeling, with her service revolver in her hand. It looked like a .38. A small pool of blood had seeped out from beneath her and now red was smeared across the concrete floor.

Tallon realized the men outside had stopped shooting. He considered their weapons. What did they have? He couldn't be sure but it sounded like shotguns and deer rifles.

The next barrage hit them just as Pitts was finally getting to her feet.

This time, the rounds hit everywhere. They caromed off the concrete floor. Shattered wood pieces from the workbench and clanged off the metal tool cart. Somewhere, a gasoline can or oil drum took a round and exploded. Flames began to flicker into life at the rear of the shop.

Tallon could see his SUV right by the front door.

"Stay here," he said to Pitts. "Don't shoot me."

He raced toward the office, keeping low and smashed through what was left of the door. A man was hiding behind the desk. He had a look of surprise on his face as Tallon shot him in the chest. He slid back down, his blood geysering onto the little refrigerator beneath the counter.

Tallon cautiously opened the front door of the office but no one fired. They must have thought he was one of their cohorts.

He kept low and made it to the passenger side of the Land Cruiser. He opened the door and slid across to the driver's side.

Shots erupted and the window next to his face exploded. He felt shards of something stab his face and neck as something hard hit him in the back of the head. He lost focus, almost went black and then he was driving the SUV forward, crashing through the remains of the garage door and fishtailing so the back of the vehicle was facing the work bench.

Tallon dove over the back seat of the SUV, kicked open the rear door and jumped out. Gunfire rang out and he felt something hit him hard, down low, and he momentarily lost his balance.

Off to his right, he saw Pitts returning fire. Shadowy figures were trying to follow Tallon's path into the shop. His eyes were seeing red and he wiped them away. His hand came away covered in blood.

He steadied himself, flipped open the

compartment on the SUV's rear floor and found his Heckler & Koch MP5. The best close-quarters weapon on the planet.

Tallon knew it was loaded so he brought it to his shoulder, stepped out, and spotted three men halfway into the repair shop. He fired in three-round bursts and two of the men went down, the other ducked backward.

With the compartment still open, Tallon grabbed the Mossberg Defender. He crabbed back to Pitts and handed the shotgun to her.

"Put that toy gun away," he said.

She holstered her .38.

"Let's take it to these bastards," she said. Pitts racked the pump on the shotgun and smiled. She knew what she was doing.

Tallon said, "I'm sure they're going around the back. Maybe you should meet them with that."

She nodded and took off for the back door.

Tallon ran to the front, threw a crowbar through the other garage door opening and waited as gunfire roared and bullets tore into the garage.

He stepped out and saw at least a half-dozen men standing behind a Ford pickup, pouring fire into the spot where he and Pitts had just been.

Tallon walked, almost casually toward them, firing as he went.

It was one thing to shoot into a building, hoping you hit something.

It was quite another to face a man with a submachine gun and have the balls to fire back.

None of these cowards did.

Two threw down their weapons.

One started to run.

The others didn't have time to do anything.

Tallon fired into the lot of them. Three-round bursts that shredded chests, eviscerated throats and ventilated skulls.

One by one, all five of them went down in a heap.

The sixth was running away, empty-handed.

Tallon let him go.

Behind him, he heard the unmistakable sound of a shotgun booming.

He ran back around the shop, called out, "It's me, don't shoot."

He turned and saw Pitts standing over the bodies of two men.

She was shaking her head as she turned to look at him. Tallon saw she was bleeding heavily from the side. Her white shirt was covered with blood.

The two men at the back of the shop had run right into multiple loads of double-aught buckshot. The results were gruesome to say the least.

"What the hell did you load this thing with?" Pitts asked, her eyes wide and her body shaking with adrenaline.

And then she collapsed.

CHAPTER TWENTY-EIGHT

New York didn't impress La Roca.

But he loved Long Island.

He could smell the ocean and he loved the big beautiful homes that sat up at the end of long, winding driveways. They were like castles. Fantasies, almost.

How nice would it be to live out here and be so close to the ocean and the big city? New York City was so close but you would never know it. Now, he felt like he was in a living postcard, or a television show.

It didn't feel real, but somehow, it felt so *right*.

If La Roca had to live in America, he would choose this place right here: Long Island.

Unfortunately, he knew that wouldn't be any time soon. He felt the dream nearly die within him, like a candle snuffed out by a strong breeze. It flickered back, but not as strong as before.

It was not the time.

He had to take care of business.

No, he was here to perform his duties for the cartel and as he cruised the big Buick, now loaded with more cash and drugs than he cared to think about, his focus returned.

To get caught by the police with this? He would never see the sunshine again. Never see Long Island again.

He felt the start of an erection as he thought about prison, and the men he could make do whatever he wanted them to do.

No time to think about that even though the idea brought him no small amount of guilty pleasure.

He wasn't going to prison.

And he wasn't going to daydream about living in America.

What he was going to do was take revenge for his Jefe.

CHAPTER TWENTY-NINE

"**I**s this some sort of competition?"

Pauling looked down at Tallon. He was in his hospital bed, half-inclined, and it looked to her like he was drowsy from painkillers.

"What?" he asked.

She had taken the red eye from New York after news of the shootout in Gideon had hit the airwaves and she'd received multiple messages from friends and contacts within the law enforcement community.

"I said, is this some kind of competition?" she repeated. "As in, I get shot and you have to nurse me so now you go out and get yourself shot, too. Maybe you needed a role reversal?"

He gave a lopsided smile. "Yep, that's it."

She leaned down and kissed him. His lips were dry.

"Thanks," he said.

Pauling knew he meant for her getting there so fast, probably not the smooch.

"Pitts?" he asked.

"She's doing fine." The local cops and several detectives from ISP had already filled Pauling in on the fate of Tallon's temporary partner. She'd taken a bullet to the side that had broken two ribs and exited at an opposite angle. The good news was the ribs had deflected the bullet from hitting any organs. The bad news was there had been a fair amount of damage to the bones and flesh. It would be a long, slow and painful recovery.

Tallon's wounds were much less severe. A bullet had grazed the back of his head and another one had ricocheted off his hip. Both were shallow grooves in his flesh and nothing had been broken. The shards of glass in his face were a little different. It had taken surgeons nearly two hours to remove the pieces and he had a series of small bandages over parts of his face.

"You look like you stuck your face in a beehive," Pauling said.

"Feels like it, too."

She paused. "I'm sorry about Manny."

"Yeah."

Tallon closed his eyes and Pauling put her hand on his shoulder. "ISP was very clear with me: they want us out. I'm under strict orders to bring you back to New York with me as soon as you're able to travel, which your doctor said is tomorrow."

He started to protest and she cut him off. "I'm in agreement with them. They want to question you about your role in the gun battle before you leave. You'll need to make your sworn statements and then they want us gone."

"But–"

"Michael, listen to me. ISP identified the bodies at the repair shop. They belong to a white supremacist group called Viele Waffen. Pitts was working that angle, right?"

Tallon nodded and half-shrugged. He looked despondent.

"ISP feels they have enough to pin the murder of Manny, the three women, and the attempted murder of you on this white power group," Pauling explained. "Apparently, and admittedly this is preliminary, but they believe the shop was a front for CJNG and that the neo-Nazis had either tried to move in on their business, or rob them. Or both."

She looked out the window. A narrow highway road cut between two farm fields where circular hay bales had been rolled.

"Your friend may have been asking too many questions," she continued. "The safe behind the vending machine opened up a whole host of possibilities. Interesting that it was empty, though."

An expression crossed Tallon's face that told Pauling he was either angry about something or in disagreement.

"What?"

When he spoke, his voice was soft.

"No way those skinheads could've taken down Manny. They must have had help."

"Like who?"

Another half-shrug.

"I don't know."

CHAPTER THIRTY

oose ends.

That's what it always came down to. When guys like him were caught, 99.9% of the time it was because one single loose end had not been tied off neatly and it had come back to bite them in the ass.

The man who occasionally called himself Reacher was all about tying up those loose ends.

Beautiful dumb Roquelle, for instance.

He'd slipped out of the office early, left the city and drove into the little village full of locals who drank too much and didn't much care what their teenage daughters were up to. He'd used yet another burner cell phone to arrange a meeting with Roquelle, and he'd picked her up and driven them both to a park where there were no security cameras.

"So what are we going to do?" she asked him. "You really screwed this up."

"I know what I'm doing."

"Really?" Roquelle turned on him. Her little face was full of fury. "Why'd you have to kill her for Christ's sake? I mean, you got plenty rough with me but I liked it."

"Yeah, I know you like it rough."

"Let me guess, you scared Tanya and it turned you on. Made you even worse."

A sly smile crossed her face. The man who occasionally referred to himself as Reacher found himself getting turned on, too.

He could tell she was a little sad. Not enough to cry. Poor Tanya, he thought, she had been such a miserable piece of shit that not even her best friend could bring herself to cry over her murder.

"It's all under control, nothing to worry about."

"Yeah, right. You're just a big man, aren't you? Big know-it-all."

She was a sexy brunette, a little wise beyond her years with a rock-hard gymnast's body and the attitude of a truck driver. They'd had plenty of fun together, especially when she was underage.

Once she started to get a little too old for him, he was able to turn her into a recruiter. The younger girls trusted her and the money wasn't bad.

"You look really hot today," he said.

She rolled her eyes and tried to act like she didn't care, but she did. He knew her like the back of his hand, which at various times he's applied to different parts of her body with great force.

He put his hand on her shoulder.

"None of them even come close to you," he said.

"What do you mean?" She glared at him and he almost laughed. She was so suspicious but also fairly transparent. A tough little town rat who'd been backed into the corner her whole life. She was loving every minute of this and failing miserably at hiding that fact.

"Satisfying me," he answered. "You're the best. And always have been."

He unbuckled his pants, grabbed her by the neck and pulled her face into his lap.

She didn't protest.

When the job was done he put his hands back on her neck.

"The best," he said and then he snapped her neck in two.

CHAPTER THIRTY-ONE

Pauling insisted Tallon ride in a wheelchair through the Indianapolis airport. He actually didn't seem to mind. It made going through security much faster and easier, and in a matter of hours they were repeating the whole process at LaGuardia. Pauling had arranged for medical transport from the airport to her apartment, which was probably overkill.

Still, by the time she got Tallon into her bed and asleep, Pauling realized how much of an ordeal it had been for him. He looked exhausted, no doubt in part thanks to the Indiana State Police investigators who had grilled him for far too long about the shooting. Any issues, Pauling later found out, were put to the side because Pitts had insisted Tallon saved her life.

If she hadn't vouched for him, Pauling figured the ISP investigators would have leaned on him much more than they did.

Now, safe and sound back in her home, Pauling got a bottle of wine, poured herself a glass, dug out her iPad and checked her email.

None of the messages required an immediate reply so she closed her email application and logged onto a law enforcement site. She ran a general query to see if anything new had developed in Gideon. Pauling figured Pitts would keep them informed, but just in case, checking the law enforcement wires wasn't a bad idea. It might keep them a step ahead.

So far, though, there was nothing.

Locally, the murder of a young girl on Long Island was making news. It appeared the girl had been killed and now her friend, another local girl, had just been reported missing. The news media was speculating that perhaps the two cases were related.

Pauling set down her iPad.

No doubt about it, she thought, the world was simply a very dangerous place.

CHAPTER THIRTY-TWO

Tallon's sweat had soaked the sheets. He was no longer in pain, but he'd just had a nightmare. In his fevered slumber, he'd seen Manny calling to him on a charred battlefield but instead of there being a rifle in his hand, there was a cell phone. And then a mortar shell exploded and Manny was blown to bits.

He awoke, felt the soggy sheets, and got out of bed. He went straight to the shower and although it was awkward with the bandages on various parts of his body, he got the job done.

In the mirror, he was amused by the scattering of wounds across his face. It looked like he had a haphazard and gruesome five o'clock shadow. Like something from a horror movie.

Tallon heard Pauling say something to him

from the other room but he was too focused. He got dressed, another slow and painful process, and emerged from the bedroom.

"What are you doing?" Pauling asked. "You're supposed to be resting."

Tallon eased himself into a comfortable chair facing Pauling. "I know, but what happened makes no sense."

Pauling set aside her iPad and made a gesture for him to continue. He knew she wanted to hear what he'd pieced together and see if it made logical sense.

"If Manny had wanted me to help, why didn't he wait?" Tallon asked. It had been bothering him from the minute he'd found his friend's body. "He sends me a text message to meet at a certain hotel a couple of hours from Gideon. But then he leaves before I get there?"

"Maybe he was impatient."

"No," Tallon said. Shaking his head. "Not his style. Even worse: he sends me the message saying he needs help, he leaves before I get there, and he gets captured, tortured and killed by a gang of Indiana neo-Nazis. Does that make any sense to you?"

"Not on a surface level," Pauling admitted. "But I also don't know what your friend's state of mind was. I mean, we're all getting older. Maybe his skills weren't what they used to be."

"I'm not talking about physical skill. I'm talking about simply from a tactical viewpoint. You only call for reinforcements if you really need them. And then, if you do decide help is necessary and you make the call, you certainly wait for it to arrive. So he made several odd decisions that resulted in his death. Or..."

The implication hung in the room.

"Or what?"

"Or, the whole thing is bullshit."

"What do you mean the whole thing?"

Outside, a city bus honked its horn and nearby, someone revved their engine. The late afternoon light streamed in from Pauling's industrial-sized windows and cast shadows in the corners.

"I mean, what if Manny didn't actually send those message to me?" Tallon reasoned. "What if someone used his cell phone or some other method to contact me. I was never able to get ahold of him on the phone. We never actually had a conversation."

"Why would they do that? And probably just as important, how?"

"I don't know. But Pitts was definitely

convinced, and the other detectives who questioned me seemed to agree, that the Mexican cartel was using that repair shop as a hub."

"So the cartel wanted you involved?"

"Maybe. I'm not sure. If there was a turf war, and the cartel knew one of their employees had a brother who was a hell of a soldier, maybe they wanted him to get involved."

"Like, fight their battle by proxy? Maybe not knowing who he was actually fighting for?"

"Yeah. Like what if they realized the skinheads had killed three of their employees and instead of sending their own soldiers to take care of them, they sent Manny? And then sent me a message to get me to go and help? I did, after all, kill quite a few of those guys."

"Seems kind of elaborate."

"I agree," Tallon admitted. "Plus, it doesn't solve the other issue."

"What's that?"

"No way those boys killed Manny by themselves. They had to have help."

"So maybe someone knew he was coming."

"Or, the cartel has a mole."

Pauling stood, crossed the room and squeezed into the chair next to Tallon. He winced a little but she was on the other hip and the warmth of her body soothed him.

"Tell you what, let's talk to a guy I know at the Bureau," Pauling said. "He's in charge of the CJNG thing. The last time he told me they were trying to get into New York. He'll know if the cartel would make these kinds of moves."

Tallon liked the sound of that. He needed to take action. He'd let the ISP chase him out of Indiana, but he'd be damned if he wasn't going to find out who killed Manny.

"What's this guy's name?"

"Roger Chinnock."

CHAPTER THIRTY-THREE

S he was in pain but Indiana State Police Detective Stevie Pitts insisted on sitting in on the questioning of one of the few members of Viele Waffen who were still alive.

Wayne Adams had lost all of the bravado she'd remembered when she'd paid a visit to the rundown farmhouse a few miles out of Gideon. Back then, he'd seemed like a twisted little emperor of a shoddy kingdom no one else would ever be interested in.

Now, he looked like a tired old beaten man.

Which was great.

The interrogation had been going on for almost an hour and he'd given up some information, but they all knew he had more to give. It was time to play hardball.

"So you think you'll do okay in prison?" Pitts asked.

His face pinched, like he'd bitten into something sour. "I'll survive."

She tilted her head. "How about that beautiful barefoot bride of yours? I know she doesn't have many teeth left, but I imagine the rest of them would get knocked out of her little hillbilly mouth at the big house. Especially if word gets out her husband is a snitch."

"You black bitch," he said to her.

"Why thank you," Pitts replied.

"She ain't done nothin' wrong."

"My point exactly!" Pitts laughed. "What an injustice it would be for her, at her age, to go off to prison. Those big old bull dykes would love to eat up a little farm girl like your wife. Especially, once they find out she was married to a Nazi, the ladies of *color* would take a real liking to her, if you know what I mean."

Pitts shot the old man a lascivious wink.

Adams seemed to shrink in on himself. "What the hell do you want?" He said it with a scowl but there was fear in his eyes. A lot of fear. Maybe even terror.

"We want the name of the man who hired you and your racist friends to do his dirty work," Pitts said. "We've got proof from all of your phone records that you were talking to someone."

"So trace the numbers," Adams said. "You've got all that newfangled technology, don't you?"

"We're working on it," Pitts lied. All the numbers were untraceable. "But it would sure speed up the process if you would stop lying and trying to protect your dead Nazi friends. Hell, they won't know if you share some information with us. They're already in Hell."

"Shit, you think he told us his name?" Adams said. "I'm the only one who figured out he was in New York."

The old man was looking down at his shoes, probably cursing his luck, so he didn't see the look of surprise flash across Pitts's face. Most of what she'd said was an educated guess, but Adams had just confirmed their suspicions.

"How did you figure out he was from New York?"

Now the old man straightened up in his chair. His face took on the look of a child who'd gotten the best of an adult. "One time I could hear an announcer in the background and knew the man was at a ball game."

Pitts felt her enthusiasm wane.

"That's it?"

"You know when they go over who's going to play at what position before the game starts?"

"Yeah."

"Well, the announcer said, "*'Your New York Yankees!'*" Adams clapped his hands together. "I said, boys, he done slipped up! Can't outsmart a country boy like me!"

Pitts scoffed. "So the big piece of information you're giving me is the guy who gave you and the rest of the Viele Waffen marching orders was in New York? A city of 14 million people? What good does that do me?"

"No, that's what I'm saying I figured out. But I wasn't the only one trying."

"What's that supposed to mean."

"One of the other boys — he's dead now so I don't mind telling you this — point blank asked our friend in New York his name but the answer don't make no sense."

"Why?"

Adams gave a look of exasperation and he spread his hands out as he asked the question.

"Because what in the hell is a Reacher?"

CHAPTER THIRTY-FOUR

Tallon emerged from the cab at the corner of Worth and Lafayette in Lower Manhattan. He'd gotten the call from Roger Chinnock that he could meet and since Pauling had left for an appointment with physical therapy, he'd decided to go alone.

He was tired and frustrated with the lack of progress but within him there was a glimmer of hope that this FBI agent could give him some intel that would help him get back in the game.

He owed it to Manny.

The sun was nearly below the horizon and there was a slight chill in the air. Since Tallon had asked for a "private" meeting – Chinnock had suggested a bench near the middle of one of the many parks in the area. Tallon was fine with that.

The more off-record this conversation would be, the better.

Whatever he learned from this meeting would be used to exact revenge. Tallon didn't believe in vigilante justice, per se, but if he had the opportunity to punish the person responsible for Manny's brutal death, he would take it.

Tallon walked down the sidewalk. His hip ached and his neck still felt stiff. The cool wind felt like a much needed astringent to help heal the gouges on his face. Already, several people had done double takes as he walked by. They probably wondered if he was wearing a mask. Or playing a part in a movie.

He wondered if there would be scars. At this point in his life, he didn't really care. Any sense of vanity had left him a long time ago.

As he walked, he fished his cell phone out of his pocket. He wanted to let Pauling know that he'd taken her suggestion and was about to meet with Chinnock.

He passed the mouth of an alley and too late realized he'd passed a shadow that suddenly moved and he felt a piercing sensation in the middle of his back as over fifty thousand volts shocked his body.

Tallon collapsed to the pavement and the last

thing he saw before blackness overtook him was a brief flash of bright red hair, cut very short.

CHAPTER THIRTY-FIVE

As often as the world bemoaned the digitization of society and the intrusiveness of modern living, many of the conveniences it provided were taken for granted.

For those with a working knowledge of internet search engines it was very easy to place "alerts" for certain words. This way, breaking news on any particular topic of interest would be automatically sent to their attention.

Much earlier and on a much more precise scale, the FBI had pioneered a similar search method for its criminal investigators. Certain search terms could be identified and then when those words, names or phrases were entered into a collection of law enforcement databases via many different methods, the investigator would be notified.

Although she was no longer in the FBI, Pauling had managed to maintain access to the Bureau's databases and take advantage of search term alerts.

Among the terms she kept tabs on was *Jack Reacher*. She had done so initially for very personal reasons; she had once been very close to him and for a long time hoped he would come back into her life.

He never had.

Later, after she realized Reacher was a man for the open road, she had considered ending the alert. She never got around to it because deep down, she thought Reacher might be a good man to keep tabs on for a whole host of reasons.

Now, back at her apartment after another grueling physical therapy session, she was surprised to see Tallon had gone. She shook her head. The man was pushing it too hard, too fast.

Pauling took a quick shower, changed and decided to get some work done. She fired up her laptop and the first thing she saw was a notification that "Reacher" had been entered into two new crime reports.

Scanning the information before her, Pauling

realized it made no sense. She looked at the name of the person who had authored the first entry. A cop on Long Island.

Pauling skipped down to the second entry.

Pauling was shocked yet again.

She recognized the name.

Indiana State Police Detective Stevie Pitts.

Pauling saw there was a phone number attached to the report.

She picked up her phone and punched in the number for Pitts.

CHAPTER THIRTY-SIX

FBI Special Agent Roger Chinnock was in a fine mood. His fun little hobby of referring to himself as "Reacher" made life so entertaining.

For instance, now, to be meeting with that bitch Lauren Pauling's current beau was immensely amusing to him. He'd really hoped this Tallon idiot would have been killed in Indiana.

Oh well.

He sat on the park bench and felt the cool chill of the air. Winter was coming. *If I'm cold, think of how cold Roquelle is*, he thought and laughed.

It was so rude of him to kill her right after she'd orally pleasured him. Where were his manners? *I really ought to rethink my treatment of women*, he thought and laughed again.

He pushed aside his merriment and focused on the task at hand: loose ends. So important! Things hadn't gone the way he would have liked in Indiana. His goal had been to send the cartel a message. When he'd seen that the brother of one of the cartel's mules was a good buddy of Michael Tallon – the same Michael Tallon he'd heard was Lauren Pauling's significant other – the opportunity had been too good to pass up.

He'd hated Pauling ever since he'd trained under her and vowed to get even with her. Everything she'd done back then she claimed was just part of the job. But at times, he felt embarrassed and humiliated when she discovered he'd made a mistake. He'd always had trouble letting things go, especially if the slights were made by a woman.

So when he had illegally gained access to Pauling's personnel file and read all about her history with this Jack Reacher character, it had presented another opportunity he couldn't let go by. It had become second nature whenever he needed to give an alias while he was doing something horribly wrong, to automatically use the Reacher name. It never got old!

His little project in Indiana had been pure genius. He'd manipulated the skinheads to ambush Manny Ordonez, and had them send a message to Tallon. That way, either Tallon or the Waffen would die. In a perfect world, it would have been both. The cartel would've gotten the message, his co-conspirators would be dead, and Pauling would be heartbroken.

Everything tied up in a neat bow with no links back to him.

But things hadn't totally gone to plan. Tallon and an ISP detective had gotten the best of the Indiana neo-Nazis. He supposed he should have seen that coming. Ah, no use second-guessing himself now.

Now, Roger realized he had his work cut out for him.

Things had just gotten a little out of control. His need for fresh young girls had grown even more urgent and gotten him into some trouble, so much so that he'd been left with no choice but to go on the payroll of the CJNG.

Which was fine with him, but he also didn't want to be their little bitch. So he orchestrated the fiasco in Indiana to remind the cartel who held the *real* power.

It was just a matter of tying up a few loose ends.

He checked his watch. This Tallon jerk was late. Chinnock was about to get up and leave when the man slid onto the bench next to him.

"Better late than never," he said to Tallon.

But it wasn't Michael Tallon.

Although Roger Chinnock had never met Michael Tallon, he knew without a doubt the man seated next to him was not the person he'd agreed to meet.

As the knife blade flashed across his vision, Chinnock thought he was facing one of the ugliest human beings he'd ever seen. A gruesome, big-boned face, misshapen and all out of proportion looked at him with an expression completely devoid of emotion.

Chinnock registered the dark skin, dark eyes and shiny black hair, and a name popped into his head, just as the blade sliced his throat from ear to ear. The sound of the metal's edge scraping across the vertebrae in his neck registered only briefly.

The name was the final, sole occupier of Roger Chinnock's mind in the last seconds of his life.

La Roca.

CHAPTER THIRTY-SEVEN

The lights were dim.

The conference room table was made of black onyx and the recessed lights in the ceiling created matching cones of light below.

Pauling sat in one chair, next to Michael Tallon. She had her hand on his shoulder.

Across from them, Special Agent Nicky Friselle sat with a look of concern.

"It may not have been the justice you were looking for, but justice was served," she said.

Pauling hated being in the conference room. Friselle had called, requested she come immediately to the FBI's headquarters, that they had Michael Tallon in custody.

"Hardly," Pauling countered. "You *knew* the

cartel was coming for Chinnock, I get that. The question is, did you tip them off? Did you discover at some point one of your agents was double-crossing the cartel to help fund his predilection for raping and killing young women?"

Nicky's eyes subtly shifted toward the back wall of the room. Pauling knew it was two-way glass and her old friend's superiors were back there, judging the agent on her ability to walk a tightrope. Nicky's instructions had probably been to tell Pauling and Tallon just enough to get them to quietly walk away, but not implicate the Bureau in anything that had happened.

"We were about to apprehend Agent Chinnock ourselves, which is why I subdued Mr. Tallon," Nicky said. Her tone was flat and even as if she was reading from a script, which she probably was. "But before we were able to take him into custody, he was murdered by an unknown assailant."

"Who got away!" Tallon exclaimed. "Jesus, how incompetent do you have to be to let the killer of a guy you're about to arrest get away?"

"Unless you were never going to arrest Chinnock, or the cartel's hitman," Pauling pointed out. "One took care of the other, right?"

"Like I said, we were about to take Agent

Chinnock into custody," Nicky said, ignoring Pauling's implication. "He was murdered, and we are actively searching for the perpetrator. We are following up on some very promising leads."

"And in the meantime, Manny Ordonez was killed, I almost died and Detective Pitts in Indiana almost died, too," Tallon said. It was hard to keep the anger out of his voice. "Three innocent people caught up in this mess."

"Mr. Ordonez tried to take the law into his own hands–"

"Wow, could you be any more hypocritical?" Tallon asked.

"–Detective Pitts was working the case and was wounded in the line of duty."

A silence fell over the room. Pauling knew her friend was between a rock and a hard place, but the tactics of the Bureau sometimes made her skin crawl.

"So what do you want from us?" Pauling finally asked.

"Just a simple reassurance that you are confident the Bureau and the Indiana State Police can take it from here. Once we have that, you are free to go."

"And if not?"

Nicky's expression faltered. The artificial

compassion was gone, and the steely resolve she was legendary for appeared. "Come on, Lauren," she said, her voice no longer soft. Instead, it was forceful. "Do you really want me to go there? Is that your goal?"

Pauling immediately knew what she meant. Tallon had killed no small amount of people in Indiana. Granted, it was self-defense and the victims were criminals. However, the Bureau had an arsenal of attorneys; prosecutors who could make the most outlandish scenarios seem plausible and if the evidence was controlled by the FBI, it could be manipulated by them, too.

Don't make me go there. Nicky didn't want to have to actually express the threat that the Bureau could make Tallon's life a living hell. Maybe even get him some prison time. Or, they could certainly do enough damage to him professionally that he would never work again.

And for what?

The man responsible for Manny Ordonez's death was dead.

There was nothing here to win and plenty to lose.

"Sounds like it's all in good hands," Tallon said, making the decision for both himself and

Pauling. His voice was heavy with sarcasm. He got to his feet a bit unsteadily.

"Yeah, I agree," Pauling said. "Good luck catching the guy who killed Roger. I'm sure we'll see it on the news very, very soon."

Nicky regained her composure and smiled.

"Great. You know your way out?"

CHAPTER THIRTY-EIGHT

As the only male agent in the small Long Island real estate company, Ed Briscoll often accompanied his female counterparts on showings where they felt unsafe. It was a professional courtesy, of course, as female agents were often targets for assault by men posing as buyers. It was an easy way to get a woman alone in an empty house.

For the first time in his professional life, though, it was Ed who felt unsafe. Despite the fact that he was a big man, at least three inches over six feet and with the solid build of a former athlete, he suddenly felt queasy.

It was because of his client.

The man who'd just agreed to buy the big colonial house, high on a hill with a long winding driveway. The property was classic Long Island with a great view.

But the man?

The man was strange, to say the least.

He had said not a single word as he toured the house and when he was done, he'd simply told Ed, "I buy."

The way his voice had sounded sent shivers down Ed's expansive back. He carried with him a boilerplate offer sheet and now, after he'd filled in the offer, which was for the full asking price, he held it out to the man to sign.

The client took the pen and clipboard in hand and slowly added his signature, lowering his head to do so.

Ed couldn't tear his eyes away from the sight of the enormous skull before him.

It was a huge melon of a head, with weird bulges and craters that seemed to shift like plates of concrete down the side of his face.

Ed, still in slight physical fear, tried to imagine what it would feel like to punch his client in the jaw in self-defense.

It would probably feel like hitting a rock.

THE END

BUY THE NEXT BOOK IN THE SERIES! THE JACK REACHER CASES - BOOK 14!

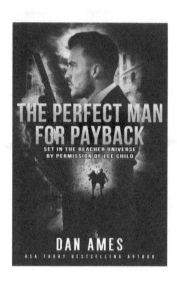

CLICK HERE TO BUY NOW!

THE FIRST BOOK IN THE SERIES...

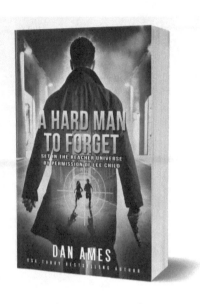

Book One in The JACK REACHER Cases

CLICK HERE TO BUY NOW

START A NEW JACK REACHER SERIES!

CLICK HERE TO BUY NOW!

A FAST-PACED ACTION-PACKED THRILLER SERIES

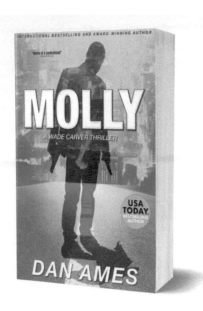

CLICK HERE TO BUY

AN AWARD-WINNING BESTSELLING MYSTERY SERIES

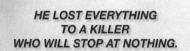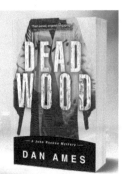

Buy DEAD WOOD, the first John Rockne Mystery.

CLICK HERE TO BUY

"Fast-paced, engaging, original."

-NYTimes bestselling author Thomas Perry

ALSO BY DAN AMES

THE JACK REACHER CASES

The JACK REACHER Cases #1 (A Hard Man To Forget)

The JACK REACHER Cases #2 (The Right Man For Revenge)

The JACK REACHER Cases #3 (A Man Made For Killing)

The JACK REACHER Cases #4 (The Last Man To Murder)

The JACK REACHER Cases #5 (The Man With No Mercy)

The JACK REACHER Cases #6 (A Man Out For Blood)

The Jack Reacher Cases #7 (A Man Beyond The Law)

The JACK REACHER Cases #8 (The Man Who Walks Away)

The JACK REACHER Cases (The Man Who Strikes Fear)

The JACK REACHER Cases (The Man Who Stands Tall)

The JACK REACHER Cases (The Man Who Works Alone)

The Jack Reacher Cases (A Man Built For Justice)

The Jack Reacher Cases #13 (A Man Born For Battle)

The Jack Reacher Cases #14 (The Perfect Man For Payback)

The Jack Reacher Cases #15 (The Man Whose Aim Is True)

The Jack Reacher Cases #16 (The Man Who Dies Here)

The Jack Reacher Cases #17 (A Man With Nothing To Lose)

The Jack Reacher Cases #18 (The Man Who Never Goes Back)

JACK REACHER'S SPECIAL INVESTIGATORS

DEAD MEN WALKING (Jack Reacher's Special Investigators #1)

GAME OVER (Jack Reacher's Special Investigators #2)

LIGHTS OUT (Jack Reacher's Special Investigators #3)

NEVER FORGIVE, NEVER FORGET (Jack Reacher's Special Investigators #4)

HIT THEM FAST, HIT THEM HARD (Jack Reacher's Special Investigators #5)

THE JOHN ROCKNE MYSTERIES

DEAD WOOD (John Rockne Mystery #1)

HARD ROCK (John Rockne Mystery #2)

COLD JADE (John Rockne Mystery #3)

LONG SHOT (John Rockne Mystery #4)

EASY PREY (John Rockne Mystery #5)

BODY BLOW (John Rockne Mystery #6)

THE WADE CARVER THRILLERS

MOLLY (Wade Carver Thriller #1)

SUGAR (Wade Carver Thriller #2)

ANGEL (Wade Carver Thriller #3)

THE WALLACE MACK THRILLERS

THE KILLING LEAGUE (Wallace Mack Thriller #1)

THE MURDER STORE (Wallace Mack Thriller #2)

FINDERS KILLERS (Wallace Mack Thriller #3)

THE MARY COOPER MYSTERIES

DEATH BY SARCASM (Mary Cooper Mystery #1)

MURDER WITH SARCASTIC INTENT (Mary Cooper Mystery #2)

GROSS SARCASTIC HOMICIDE (Mary Cooper Mystery #3)

THE CIRCUIT RIDER WESTERNS

THE CIRCUIT RIDER (Circuit Rider #1)

KILLER'S DRAW (Circuit Rider #2)

RAY MITCHELL THRILLERS

THE RECRUITER

KILLING THE RAT

HEAD SHOT

ANGEL PIKE THRILLERS

Angel To Fear

Angel of Truth

Angel of Justice

Angel Without Mercy

STANDALONE BOOKS & STORIES

KILLER GROOVE (Rockne & Cooper Mystery #1)

BEER MONEY (Burr Ashland Mystery #1)

TO FIND A MOUNTAIN (A WWII Thriller)

BOX SETS

JACK REACHER CASES 1-03

JACK REACHER CASES 4-6

JACK REACHER CASES 7-9

JACK REACHER CASES 10-12

JACK REACHER CASES 13-15

AMES TO KILL

GROSSE POINTE PULP

GROSSE POINTE PULP 2

TOTAL SARCASM

WALLACE MACK THRILLER COLLECTION

SHORT STORIES:

THE GARBAGE COLLECTOR

BULLET RIVER

SCHOOL GIRL

HANGING CURVE

SCALE OF JUSTICE

MISS JANUARY (PIN-UP MYSTERY #1)

MISS FEBRUARY (PIN-UP MYSTERY #2)

MISS MARCH (PIN-UP MYSTERY #3)

MISS APRIL (PIN-UP MYSTERY #4)

MISS MAY (PIN-UP MYSTERY #5)

MURDER LAKE

SAVAGE LAKE

ABOUT THE AUTHOR

Dan Ames is a USA TODAY Bestselling Author, Amazon Kindle #1 bestseller and winner of the Independent Book Award for Crime Fiction.

www.authordanames.com
dan@authordanames.com

FREE BOOKS AND MORE

**Would you like a FREE copy
of my story BULLET RIVER and the
chance
to win a free Kindle?**

**Then sign up for the DAN AMES BOOK
CLUB:**

For special offers and new releases, sign up here

THE PERFECT MAN FOR PAYBACK

The Jack Reacher Cases #14

A USA TODAY BESTSELLING BOOK

Book One in The JACK REACHER Cases

AuthorDanAmes.com

PRAISE FOR DAN AMES

"Fast-paced, engaging, original."

— NEW YORK TIMES
BESTSELLING AUTHOR
THOMAS PERRY

"Ames is a sensation among readers who love fast-paced thrillers."

— MYSTERY TRIBUNE

"Cuts like a knife."

— SAVANNAH MORNING NEWS

"Furiously paced. Great action."

— NEW YORK TIMES
BESTSELLING AUTHOR BEN
LIEBERMAN

FREE BOOKS AND MORE

**Would you like a FREE copy
of my story BULLET RIVER and the
chance
to win a free Kindle?**

Then sign up for the DAN AMES BOOK CLUB:

AuthorDanAmes.com

NEW SERIES! JACK REACHER'S SPECIAL INVESTIGATORS.

AuthorDanAmes.com

THE PERFECT MAN FOR PAYBACK

The Jack Reacher Cases #14

by

Dan Ames

"The axe forgets, but the tree remembers."

-African proverb

CHAPTER ONE

The medium-security federal prison sat baking under the harsh Oklahoma sun. The sky was cloudless. Even birds avoided the unmistakable scent of loss and desperation hanging over the cinderblock and razor-wired structure.

In Cell Block D, Michael "Stone" Morticelli studied his face in the mirror. His olive complexion had deepened into a dark tan, and his blue eyes blazed out from the reflection in the glass.

He'd been inside for less than two years now and he'd never looked better, he realized, even though he wasn't a vain man. With little to do other than read and exercise, both his body and mind had sharpened immeasurably. He had the upper body of a stone mason, which is what his trade had been as a very young man in his father's business. This was all well before he'd graduated to the *other* family business. It was how he'd gotten his nickname, as well.

His neck was thick, his shoulders broad and his arms taut with muscle. Even his large hands gave the appearance of strength and something more sinister. Early in his career he'd strictly performed enforcer work. It was something he'd enjoyed and for which he clearly showed an apti-tude. Success changes things, of course, and soon he was rising through the ranks of the Barranca crime family.

Until that day when everything changed.

He pushed those memories aside for they did him no good. Now, the steam from the shower had coated the mirror's glass with a thin mist and he wiped it away. As he did, the reflection changed.

His face was not the only one in the mirror.

Stone turned and faced the two men who had silently appeared behind him.

The prison was medium security and most inmates were not violent. But within the walls there were a few dangerous men.

The two individuals facing Stone were widely

considered to be at the top of the food chain. Perhaps just under Stone himself.

They were twin brothers. Niko and Tre Theodopolus. Rumored to be hitmen for a Corsican gang in New York, they were to be feared and avoided. Like most twins, they kept to themselves, rarely spoke to others, and rarely even spoke to each other.

Stone wasn't surprised to see them. He'd been expecting this day would come ever since he'd landed in prison. If anything, he wondered why now. It'd been no small amount of time since his conviction and he had begun to wonder if the parties responsible for putting him in prison had decided he was no longer a threat.

Clearly, they did.

Life in prison is a balancing act, a series of unwritten rules most inmates follow. Stone knew them as well as everyone else, and he also knew that he had not made enemies. There had been no fights. No disputes. He kept to himself.

So the appearance of the twins had nothing do with what had happened within the walls. Rather, they were here because of forces *outside* the walls.

Although both of the men facing him were taller than Stone, he outweighed them each by at least twenty pounds. They didn't have his bulk; rather, they were slender like athletes, all sinew and bone. They would be quick, rather than powerful.

That didn't bother Stone.

It was the crude knife each of them held in his hand that gave him pause. He wondered how they would attack. Simultaneously? Or would the alpha of the pair strike first?

The answer, when it came, was fairly obvious.

The twins acted at the same time.

They lunged forward, both with the same expression – a grimace that almost seemed like a smile.

Stone's hand lashed out to his left where a three-foot-long towel bar, made of iron, had been bolted to the concrete wall. He'd been shaving in front of the same mirror for nearly two years and over time, had noticed the bolts holding the bar in place were corroding. He'd gently loosened them over time and now his enormous hand gripped the bar and ripped it from the wall as he dodged to his left. That put one of the twins in front, the other behind.

Stone pivoted and swung the bar on a short arc. The first brother's knife whisked past Stone's chest just as the iron bar connected with the man's temple. It sounded like a baseball bat hitting a ball into deep centerfield. Stone felt the crush of the iron all through his arm.

The first of the Corsican brothers sagged and folded to the bathroom floor, his shiv clattering along the tile.

The second brother stepped in and thrust his shiv forward, opting for a direct stab. Stone had already pivoted back and this time, the pipe came via backhand and connected with the attacker's wrist. Stone heard bones break and the home-made blade went airborne, landing somewhere near the showers.

Stone dropped the iron bar as the second brother hurled himself forward. If he'd been worried before, now, all fear was gone. Close quarters fighting with no weapons other than hands was his forte.

Stone ducked his head, felt the man's fists bounce off his midsection and he caught the remaining twin's neck in his hands. He wrenched his forearms and heard the Corsican's neck snap. The man's body went limp and Stone held him, practically airborne for a few seconds and then he let go and the body dropped. It reminded Stone of dropping a trash bag into the bin.

Stone walked over to where the iron bar lay on

the floor, picked it up, and went to the first brother, who was still breathing. Stone raised the bar and smashed it down, crushing the Corsican's skull.

The man stopped breathing.

Stone dropped the pipe to the floor.

He didn't have much time.

This wasn't the end of it.

It was only the beginning.

And now, he had to activate the plan he'd put in place immediately after his arrival and had only needed the spark to set it in motion.

The fact they'd come for him now, after all this time, meant he had only one option.

Escape.

CHAPTER TWO

The wiry old man held the knife, a stiletto, pointed directly at Lauren Pauling. He was dressed all in black and his skin was dark brown. His shoes were black and he seemed to float above the floor. His close-cropped silver hair seemed to glow in the dim light of the room. His eyes were dark pools of blackness, showing no emotion, just cold, calculated cunning.

Pauling kept her breath steady, let the flow of the fight come to her. She'd trained before in a variety of weapon styles and knew not to panic. Let things come naturally.

The man thrust forward, a move of liquid poetry, and Pauling's own knife slashed forward seemingly of its own volition, down and then through. She hadn't thought about the move, it just happened. Simultaneously, she caught the old man's forearm in her free hand and reversed her knife's path, slashing along his stomach.

Pauling stepped back and the man straightened.

"Very good," he said in his heavily accented English.

He looked at his wrist. The knives were trainers - made of rubber - but Pauling's "blade" had left a red mark on his inner arm, barely visible on the dark skin. Pauling felt a twinge of guilt as her "opponent" was so much older, she figured he might be nearly eighty years old. But he was lean, and his body didn't look like an old man's. He moved with an easy grace of a natural athlete.

She knew him only by the name Accursio, which made her always wonder if he was prone to swearing, or foul language.

Pauling didn't know much more than that, save for the fact he was a world-renowned knife fighter in the Sicilian tradition of fighting with stilettos. An old friend in the Bureau, also retired, had recommended him to Pauling after she'd claimed she was looking for something new.

"You must always remember angles," Accursio

now said to her. "Some say it is a triangle." He pointed to the floor and outlined a pattern by her feet, showing her various approaches of attack. "But it is wasted energy to focus too much on this. Remember, it is the angle that wins, not the blade."

They went through several more moves as the ancient Sicilian tweaked her footwork, challenged her balance and several times placed the tip of his rubber knife directly into the skin over her heart.

Training is humility, she told herself.

By the end, she had worked up a good sweat and realized she was happy. As if she'd just seen a good movie or experienced something deeply satisfying.

"I will see you two days from now," Accursio told her. There was no set schedule. He simply instructed when she should come back to his basement studio.

Pauling gathered her workout bag and bottled water. As she was heading for the door, Accursio said her name, softly.

The workout facility was in the basement of a butcher shop on Manhattan's Lower East Side. Pauling had no idea if her instructor owned the building, or the shop, but the room was silent.

"Pardon me?" Pauling said.

"You should be careful," he said.

"Yes," she replied. "Being aware is the best defense."

"No. You do not understand," he said.

Pauling turned and gazed at the old man. He was standing with his hands by his sides. His dark eyes were fixed on her.

"You understand where I am from?" he asked.

"Yes, of course."

"You know silence is the treasure of Sicily."

Pauling waited.

Accursio walked toward her. He held out his hand. In his palm was a 9-inch Sicilian stiletto. It was a folded blade, released by a button. She didn't know what kind of handle it was, but it looked like old ivory. Pauling knew it was the real thing, the blade would be razor-sharp.

"You are not here by accident, I believe," he said. "This is how things work."

"Thank you," she said. "But why do I need to be careful?" she asked. Pauling slipped the knife into her pocket.

"A man who locks his hate away is a fool, for one day, it will break free."

He nodded to the door.

When she opened it and turned back to say goodbye, he was already gone.

CHAPTER THREE

The beauty of La Cosa Nostra or "our thing" as the Mafia referred to themselves, was the sheer numbers. Any army's strength is judged by the number of soldiers within its ranks. The same is true of any criminal organization and the Mob had been around a long time, securing its thirsty tentacles to all forms of commerce for over a century.

Prison, as well, had its own type of commerce.

Almost all of it illicit and vulnerable to exploitation.

The head guard of Cell Block D in the medium-security institution home, for the moment, to Stone Morticelli, had been "gotten to" by the Italians. His name was Bud Dupree and he had a fondness for methamphetamine and females around the age of puberty. A large stash of illegal drugs and a set of photographs worthy of the label 'child pornography' had been combined with a threat to tell Bud's wife and the warden.

The threat had been more than enough to bring Bud Dupree into the fold of the Mafia. Stone had been made well aware of Dupree's compromised position and filed it away for future use.

That time was now.

Stone hurriedly dressed, then walked quickly from the bathroom to the guard office. The space was separated by a single, steel-framed door with shatterproof glass. There was an intercom next to the door. Beyond the door was a small room, a perfect square, with a desk that ran along one wall, and atop the desk were a number of video camera feeds.

Bud Dupree glanced up and then frowned. He was large, slow-moving, with a scruffy beard and tired eyes. Dupree's lifestyle of drugs and booze showed; he was fair-haired and freckled, but his cheeks were red with hypertension and his belly hung over his belt.

Stone watched him as he leaned forward in his chair and pressed a button near the camera system's control board.

"What 'n hell do you want?" Dupree asked with his unmistakable southern drawl.

Stone held up his hands and let his eyes find the camera pointing down at him.

A look crossed Bud's face and Stone knew the man understood. The overweight guard begrudgingly got to his feet, scooped a set of prison cuffs from the counter and came to the door. Stone obediently stepped back six feet and let Bud open the door.

Wisely, the guard didn't shut the door.

He clamped a cuff on Stone's left wrist and then did the same with his right, except instead of the cuff clicking shut, it made a muted sound and Stone knew Bud had slipped his finger in between, preventing the cuff from closing. He'd used his body to shield the action from the camera, and now, he pulled Stone through.

Stone heard Bud whisper over his left shoulder.

"Shit, man. You tryin' to get me fired?"

"Absolutely not," Stone said. "Just take me to the doc and I'll explain everything. It's going to be fine."

"Better be," Dupree said.

Like all prisoners, Stone had spent many countless hours studying the habits and practices

of the prison. Being medium-security, there were
a lot fewer secrets than in the big houses.

Many of the inmates were older, white-collar
criminals prone to all sorts of medical maladies.
Bunions, gout, ulcers and diabetes.

Stone also knew the doctor was only at the
prison on Mondays and Thursdays. This being a
Friday, the office would be empty.

Bud led his charge through the hallway
between the main prison blocks and through
another set of doors that housed the administra-
tive sections. The doctor's office was at the end of
the hall.

The security guard unlocked the door and he
pushed Stone through.

Once the door was closed, Stone took off the
cuff and bud quickly unlocked the one on his
right wrist.

"Please tell me you need drugs," Bud said.
"Booze. A hooker."

"Sorry," Stone said. "I just killed the twins."

The blood drained from Bud's red face. "Both
of them?"

Stone nodded.

"Why?"

"Why do you think? They came for me." He

studied Bud's face and then said, "Take off your uniform."

"No way," the man shook his head. Stone could see tufts of red hair sticking out from underneath the prison-issued baseball cap. "Nuh uh."

Bud Dupree was a big man and Stone didn't relish the idea of trying to take off the man's uniform if he was unconscious.

"I'm going to give you a little tap on the side of the head before I leave," Stone replied. "You'll be able to say I got the jump on you." He slid one of the shiv's from the Corsican brothers. He held it in front of him and Dupree knew he had no choice.

"Ah, shit," Bud said. He hurriedly removed his shirt and pants along with his keys.

Stone waited until he was done then threw a short right cross that caught the guard on the side of the jaw. A horrible grinding sound, followed by a pop, filled the room.

Stone grimaced.

Bud sagged to the floor and cracked his head on the tile.

It was better this way, Stone thought. He hadn't wanted to tell Bud that he needed his wallet and car keys. Or what he planned to do afterward.

Stone knew exactly where Bud's car was parked and the exit protocol.

He threw on the guard's uniform, pocketed the cash from the wallet, grabbed the keys and left the shiv that he'd promised Bud. The gun crammed in a snap-on leather holster was a lame-ass .38. Stone shook his head.

Amateur hour, he thought.

Stone studied Dupree's face – the eyes were open and the big man's chest was still.

"Damn it," Stone said. He leaned down and felt the man's neck. Even through the fat and double chin, it was clear there was no pulse.

Stone realized he'd just killed a prison guard, a civilian, and unofficially on the Mob's payroll.

"This is just getting worse," he said.

He slipped the .38 into his pocket, put on the ball cap and pulled it down over his face. He peeked out the door. The hallway was empty.

Stone left the doctor's office and tried to imitate Bud Dupree's unhurried strolling gait.

Down the stairs and out through the employ-ee's entrance, Stone spotted Bud's car, went to it and climbed inside. He fired up the engine, pulled the guard's cap even lower over his face and drove up to the prison gate. It opened automatically and Stone drove through, giving a half-hearted wave to the guard operating the door.

The man waved back.

Moments later, he was roaring down the Oklahoma highway, with a very specific destination in mind.

CHAPTER FOUR

P auling thought about Accursio's strange comment at the end of their training session.

Something about a man locking his hate away and then it breaking free.

What was it with old people always speaking in parables, she wondered. Maybe it was just the ramblings of an old man. As good as Accursio was with a knife, maybe his cognitive faculties were declining. He could be suffering from the onset of dementia.

Pauling crossed the street and walked toward her building on Barrow Street. She felt great. Working out in any kind of martial art or combat training always relaxed her, for some odd reason. It was so much better than logging miles on a treadmill. It used the mind and the body as well as muscles that were rarely used. It was also interesting that she had a nine-inch stiletto in her purse. Knife laws in New York were a bit murky but it was a short walk to her building and once home, she'd find a good place for it. She had no intention of carrying a Sicilian stiletto around on her daily activities.

The front entrance to her building on Barrow Street was highly secure, with a keypad and a second interior door, all monitored by video. The structure was an old building, a former warehouse, that had been converted into loft-style apartments and condos. She had chosen it mostly because it was only two blocks from her office. Now that she had sold her firm, that convenience was gone. But she still loved the place.

Pauling entered the lobby and immediately noticed the man in the dark suit.

If ever someone fit the image of an FBI agent, this was the guy. Tall, square-shouldered with excellent posture and the air of law enforcement. Probably in his late thirties. A senior agent, but not yet in upper management.

He stood and approached her.

"Lauren Pauling?" he asked.

"Yes."

He withdrew a leather case from the inside pocket of his jacket and showed her his Bureau badge. For a brief moment she thought about flashing the stiletto at him as a joke to see how he would respond, but resisted the impulse. Active duty Feds weren't known for their senses of humor.

She caught the name Helm on the credentials.

"I'm Agent Helm with the New York office. Do you think we could speak for a moment?" His voice was a deep baritone, full of confidence. It would serve him well in the Bureau, she thought.

Pauling lifted her chin toward the cushioned bench near the elevators. "Sure. Let's talk here."

She wasn't a big fan of bringing people up to her personal living space.

Helm hesitated, probably desiring a place more private, but then acquiesced.

"I'm really only here to deliver a preliminary message," he said.

Pauling waited.

"Do you remember Michael Morticelli? Stone Morticelli to his associates?"

"Of course."

She hadn't heard the name since she'd wrapped up the case, hadn't even thought about the man for even longer, but at the mention of his name she immediately pictured his face: a rugged man with a strong jaw, dark hair and blue eyes. Not superficially handsome but the very real element of danger in his personality added to his allure.

"We put him away awhile ago," she said. "One of my last cases. Racketeering. Conspiracy. The usual Mob stuff. Vito Barranca had been the main target, but we all know what happened to him.

Helm nodded.

Suddenly, Pauling remembered Accursio's strange comment and combined with the sudden appearance of the FBI asking questions about Stone Morticelli made sense.

"He escaped?" Pauling asked.

Helm looked surprised. "You already knew?"

"Not really."

The elevator doors opened and a woman stepped out with a miniature poodle on a leash behind her. Neither Pauling nor Helm spoke while the woman and her dog passed. The woman looked straight ahead, the poodle stared at Helm and Pauling.

"The Bureau thought it might be a good idea to let you know," Helm said. "Since you were the lead agent who put him away."

It was true, even though Pauling had been in

charge of a large team, ultimately, she was the one who had busted Morticelli and a few of his colleagues.

"Wasn't he in prison in Oklahoma?" Pauling asked.

Helm nodded. "He killed two prisoners, a guard and stole the guard's car. No one has seen him or the vehicle since."

"Any idea of his plan?"

"We're assuming revenge. He's the perfect man for payback."

Pauling knew he was right. Stone Morticelli had begun his career as a feared enforcer. One of the most dangerous and capable hitmen the Mob had ever seen. If he was loose with revenge on his mind...

Pauling pushed the thought away. She decided to try to sound positive.

"Well, you'll find him," she said. "I've got confidence in you guys."

Helm remained silent.

"Unless he has help," Pauling added.

Helm didn't say anything and avoided her gaze.

"Uh-oh," Pauling said.

CHAPTER FIVE

"Well, this is something else," the realtor said. She was a middle-aged woman with nylon slacks, colored hair and a strange perfume that Tallon thought might be a mixture of ammonia and deer scent.

It was the third time she'd said 'this is something else' and Tallon was losing his patience.

The idea to test the local real estate market with his ranch was something that had just occurred to him after his return from seeing Pauling in New York. He'd come back for a few weeks just to make sure the place was okay. And it had made him wonder about the back-and-forth.

How long was he going to keep it up?

Pauling had talked about leaving New York

and moving out here to his place right next to Death Valley, but it seemed like life always had other plans. A new case would pop up and before you knew it, they'd be back in the thick of things.

"I have to say, I've never seen a security system like this," the realtor said. She had stared at Tallon's bank of security cameras for some time and was probably wondering why the hell he needed so much surveillance equipment.

"Yes, I was robbed once, not this house, but I never forgot the feeling," Tallon lied.

He had to laugh – most of the security was hidden and she hadn't seen it. Sensors, hidden cameras, and certainly the gun safe. If he really wanted to scare her senseless, he could show her that.

"I see," she said. "Well, you have a very nice piece of land with a great view of the mountains."

"Yes, good location."

The realtor's name was Connie and now she turned to face Tallon. "The house is very nice, roomy and comfortable. Could use a woman's touch, though," she said and raised an artificially enhanced eyebrow.

Tallon wasn't serious about selling the place, at least not yet. He just wanted a ballpark number.

"Right now, we're a touch heavy on the supply side," Connie said. "But I think the right buyer might be interested."

"What price would you list the property for?" Talon asked.

Connie seemed to deliberate even though he knew she had a number in mind. Finally, she told him the price she thought the property was worth.

Tallon knew it was purposely low to guarantee a sale and earn Connie her six percent commission.

He paused and acted like it was something he would consider. "That's something I'll have to think about," he told her.

"We can always start higher and come down," she replied.

Tallon thanked her and showed her to the door.

She gave him her business card and said, "Call me. Anytime." He took the card and watched her walk out to her minivan. She had a decal on the driver's side door. Connie backed out of the driveway and drove away. Tallon saw on the back window of her minivan a bumper sticker that said "My German Shepard is smarter than your honor student."

Tallon closed the door. He knew he would not be inviting Connie back.

He walked into the kitchen, tossed the realtor's card into the trash and grabbed a cold beer from the fridge. In the backyard, he put a match to the stack of logs and kindling in the firepit and watched as it roared to life. A wave of heat pulsed out at him and the cold beer slid down his throat, settling in his stomach with a satisfying finish.

The sun began to set behind the line of mountains. A hawk circled far away, a black silhouette set against the tangerine sky.

Tallon thought about Pauling. He resisted the impulse to think that she should be here right now, next to him. That kind of thinking was bad for a relationship. The more "shoulds" that appear in your thought process, well, they're pretty much red flags indicating things aren't going well.

So he discarded any negative emotion and focused on the positive.

He knew he missed her. Still wanted to be with her.

And soon, she would either be here, or he would be back in New York.

He took another drink of beer as the hawk

disappeared behind the highest crest of the mountain.

Tallon also knew one more thing as fact.

There wasn't a chance in hell he was going to sell this ranch.

CHAPTER SIX

W*here does a wise man hide a leaf? In the forest.*

Stone Morticelli smirked, caught his own expression in the rearview mirror.

Where does an escaped convict hide a stolen car?

Its owner's house.

Stone pulled Bud Dupree's car behind the double-wide trailer the security guard owned with his wife, Sharon. Stone knew the woman's name because he'd heard Bud bitch about her constantly. Sharon this, Sharon that. It made Stone wonder why they were still married, although it was an uncomfortable thought because he himself hadn't been a paragon of marital fidelity, either. Stone had thought about his ex-wife Veronica many times, and the things they'd gone through. Veronica had divorced him during the chaos and he had not contested it.

Focusing on the task at hand, Stone steered the car, a ten-year-old Chevy, toward the address he'd memorized from Dupree's careless display of personal mail.

Hiding out at his victim's home was exactly the kind of thing most criminals on the run would never do. Stone knew the cops would come to notify Sharon that her husband was dead. He also knew that Sharon hated Bud, that her husband was never home and was a serial cheater.

Stone figured he could work with that.

He shut the engine of the car off after making sure it was completely hidden from anyone coming up the drive. The Duprees lived in the country, down a winding driveway thick with trees. No neighbors in sight.

Perfect, Stone thought.

The door to the trailer was unlocked and Stone simply let himself in. The light was dim, only the television was an intrusion into the darkness. He shut the door behind him and heard snoring.

He smelled body odor and fried food.

Stone walked into the main room of the

trailer and got his bearings. There was a kitchen at one end, a living room in the middle, and then a short hallway to a bedroom and probably a bathroom.

On the stained couch in the living room a woman was fast asleep, an empty bottle of malt liquor on the floor next to her. On the wall over the couch was a Guns N' Roses poster.

Stone walked past her into the bedroom and winced at the smell. It was like walking into a pet store.

There was a saggy bed, a cheap dresser and an open closet. Stone found Bud Dupree's meager selection of clothes on the left side. He changed out of the uniform into jeans and a T-shirt with a black leather jacket that for the most part, fit him. Stone studied the bed, saw that one side was tilted downward from weight and assumed that was the side Bud slept on. Stone went over and checked under the pillow and in the drawer of the night table.

There was nothing there.

Stone dropped to his knees and looked under the bed.

He smiled.

Stone pulled out an open soft-shell pistol case.

Inside was a .45 automatic and several spare magazines.

He put the gun in his waistband and the magazines into the pockets of the leather jacket. Stone still had the .38 but the .45 was much more his style.

Back in the living room, he searched until he found a cheap cell phone on the counter. He hoped there was no passcode to unlock it.

There wasn't.

He then dialed a number from memory.

It was the only person, male or female, he felt he could trust.

When a woman's voice answered, he gave her instructions and a deadline.

Stone knew she wouldn't miss it.

He disconnected the call, deleted the phone's call history and studied the keys on the counter. The car he'd taken from the prison was out of the question as it was the one the cops would be looking for.

Unfortunately, it didn't appear the Duprees were a two-car family.

But in addition to the keys for the Chevy, there was a key chain with a single key on it.

Stone left the phone on the counter as he knew

it could be tracked, grabbed the single key and went out to the garage. There, he found a Kawasaki 500 motorcycle and a helmet. He wasn't sure which made him more happy, the bike or the helmet. The bike was at least twenty years old and not much to look at. But the helmet would hide his face and that was just as important as transportation.

His original plan had been to force Sharon Dupree to cover for him and hide out while the cops went about their business. But the motorcycle was a stroke of luck and now he knew for sure the best way forward was to get out of Oklahoma.

He slipped on the helmet and put the key in the ignition, then walked the motorcycle all the way to the end of the driveway. He didn't want to wake Mrs. Dupree.

Praying it would start, Stone keyed the ignition and the motorcycle sputtered to life. He checked the gas tank – three-quarters full. More than enough to get him to St. Louis and the address he'd just mentioned on the phone.

Stone put the bike in gear and shot out onto the road.

It would take him less than an hour to cross the state line.

At that point, he could breathe a little easier.

CHAPTER SEVEN

"We don't know exactly that he has help," Helm said. "But he knew a lot of people."

"And I'm assuming you're monitoring their communications?" Pauling responded. They were still sitting on the bench near the elevators in her building. She saw no reason to offer her apartment as a place to continue the discussion.

"Yes."

"And?"

"Nothing yet."

"Are you monitoring all of his—"

"Pauling, you know I can't get into that. Trust me, we're doing everything we can to track him down."

Pauling got to her feet. "Okay, I appreciate

the heads-up. Let me know if there's anything I can do."

"Actually, there is," Helm said. He, too, stood and walked with Pauling toward the elevator.

"Just let us know if you see anything suspicious, anyone maybe lurking around your building or trying to contact you. I assume your home security is pretty good?"

Pauling smiled. "For what I paid? It better be."

Helm gave Pauling his card and left when the elevator doors opened. She went up to her floor, let herself into her condo and re-armed the security system. After one of her cases had gone awry a few years back, she'd paid a small fortune for a state-of-the-art security system, complete with full video, dozens of cameras and monitors, all of it backed up to a cloud-based server.

She did a quick check of the video for the hours she was out of the apartment training with Accursio.

There was nothing.

Pauling walked into her bedroom, showered and changed, then went to her computer.

She scanned the news websites for stories of Stone Morticelli's escape, but found nothing. Pauling then entered the FBI's intranet via a portal that should have been closed once she'd left the Bureau. But with help from a hacker friend, Pauling had managed to keep her access open, legally. Sort of.

There, she found the case notes on Stone's escape. He'd killed two inmates, a guard, and stolen the guard's car. Since then, no word. So, Helm had been relatively honest with her, which came as a mild surprise.

Pauling shut down her browser and checked her phone. She thought about calling Tallon, but held off. She walked into her living room and looked out the large, industrial-sized windows. Down below on the street, people went about their lives with a busy intensity. A hawk slowly cruised overhead, looking for an unsuspecting pigeon. The sky was steel gray, and a cold rain would no doubt be falling soon.

She was about to go into the kitchen when the cell phone in her hand rang. Pauling glanced at the screen, expecting to see Tallon's name.

Instead, it was an unknown number with a Chicago area code.

Alarm bells began to ring.

When Stone Morticelli had been busted, he'd been working in the family business in Chicago.

First Accursio's warning, then Agent Helm, now this.

You never know what the day is going to bring, she thought.

Pauling used her finger to swipe right, answering the call.

"Lauren Pauling?" the voice asked. It was female.

"Yes."

"Um, this is Veronica. Veronica Grasso."

The name wasn't familiar to Pauling. At least, the name Grasso. But the caller's first name, Veronica was–

"You knew me by my married name."

Pauling suddenly remembered.

"Veronica Morticelli," the woman said. "Stone's ex-wife."

CHAPTER EIGHT

The man slung the body over his shoulder and climbed the last set of stairs to the rooftop.

He pulled the door open and immediately turned to his right, away from the only spot visible to the apartment tower across the street. Hidden by the stairwell's exit door and a series of metal-clad utility structures, the man carried his load to the side of a hundred-foot-high stone cylinder from which smoke billowed.

A rectangular access panel had been built into the incinerator at the rooftop level should anyone need to dispose of waste they were unable to bring to the basement.

Which fit the man's needs perfectly.

He dropped the dead man on the rooftop's

gravel surface and heaved the access panel open. It was made of iron, heavy and rusty. A small amount of fumes gushed from the opening but the man had already ducked down to scoop up the body.

He shoved the dead man's head in first and then slid the body forward until its own weight took over and gravity pulled the rest of the load downward.

Far below, he heard the sound of the body hitting the bowels of the incinerator.

On the rooftop, the man heaved the heavy access panel door shut and turned toward the stairwell.

His phone rang.

He opened the button on his suit coat and withdrew his phone.

"Brooks," he said. The name matched the label inside his suit: Brooks Brothers. He always wore them and when he'd had to pick an alias for his employers to use, it had come readily to mind. Besides, he looked like a Brooks: classically handsome with dark hair and a strong jaw, he could have been a news anchor or a model.

Instead, he'd chosen a slightly different profession.

One that not only paid better than those but, in his opinion, held more integrity.

He listened as a familiar voice asked him to come to a meeting out in Lake Forest in two hours.

"Of course," Brooks said.

He disconnected the call and slid the phone back into its pocket.

A hundred feet above him, a new and thicker cloud of black smoke belched into the sky.

CHAPTER NINE

"Hello Veronica," Pauling said. "How can I help you?"

Pauling had already pictured the woman in her mind: very pretty, with rich chestnut hair, perfect cheekbones and a curvy body. Unlike the stereotypes most often associated with Mob wives, Veronica Morticelli had been a very classy, elegant woman. Beautiful, sophisticated and intelligent.

She had also been a key witness in the prosecution against her husband.

"I'm sure you've heard by now that Michael escaped from prison," Veronica said. "I knew medium security was a mistake."

Pauling didn't argue with the woman. She, too, had questioned the wisdom of putting Stone

Morticelli in medium security. But prison over-crowding was a huge issue and his crimes —at least the ones for which he'd been convicted — had not been violent. Although suspected of murder and murder-for-hire, those charges weren't what put him in jail, therefore, the judge had virtually no choice but to sentence him to medium security.

"Look at this way," Pauling offered. "Once he's caught, he won't be going back to a place like that. With three murder charges he'll be in maximum security. Certainly for the rest of his life. And he's bound to commit even more crimes while he's out, which hopefully won't be for long."

"I'm not worried about what happens *after* he's caught," Veronica said. "I'm worried about what he does *while* he's out."

Pauling understood what the woman was saying. She was scared. Veronica had not only testified against Stone, but had also divorced him while the case was dragging through the legal system. It was possible he hated her more than anyone else on the planet.

"Has anyone been in contact with you?" Pauling asked.

"Of course. The FBI was just here."

"Do you have your own security, too?"

Pauling knew most people like Veronica, even

loosely tied to the Mob, tended to keep a body-guard or two around, just in case.

"Yes, of course."

"Then you're in good hands."

"I asked the FBI agents who came here about you," Veronica said. "They said you're not with the Bureau anymore. Private practice, is that right?"

"Yes."

"You're private security?"

Pauling sighed. She had a feeling she knew where this was going and didn't really want to get into it.

"I was. I recently sold my firm so technically I'm unemployed."

"I'd like to change that," Veronica said. "Immediately. Name your price. I want you down here protecting me."

"I really don't think that's necessary, Veronica. The FBI has far more resources than an individ-ual, a civilian, at that."

"It's not about resources or manpower. It's about trust. I don't know these people from Adam. You, on the other hand, proved you do the right thing when it matters."

"You've got your own security in addition to

the FBI. I would just get in the way. Too many cooks in the kitchen, as they say."

"Maybe, but until Stone is caught, I want you to lead the team."

Pauling chose her words carefully. "The FBI isn't going to let me lead anything. Plus, I don't think you need me. Stone will be caught quickly. These days, it's much harder for a man like him, on the run, to stay hidden. Besides, why do you think he'd take the risk to come after you? He has to know you'll be protected by the Bureau."

"Did I ever tell you the last thing he said to me, before he got locked up?"

"No."

"He said, if it's the last thing I ever do, I'm going to strangle you with my bare hands," Veronica said. "Or die trying."

CHAPTER TEN

E ast St. Louis was nobody's idea of paradise.

But right now, in Stone Morticelli's mind, it was perfect.

Consistently ranked one of the most violent and economically depressed communities in the country, East Saint Louis was exactly what he needed; a place where no one knew him, and where an unspoken pact to not communicate with law enforcement was firmly in place.

Stone knew the Barranca family had some business in the city, every Chicago Mob family did, but he didn't think anyone here would recognize him on sight.

He parked the motorcycle near a dead-end street, removed its license plate, and dumped the plate in a garbage can. He then used most of the cash from Bud Dupree's wallet for a cheap hotel room near downtown.

There was a good chance the motorcycle would be stolen, but he didn't care.

In his room, he studied his face in the mirror. He would need to change his appearance if he could, but at the moment, he didn't have the tools he would need.

He gathered up what little cash remained, and went to a drug store around the corner. There, he had just enough to buy a disposable burner cell phone. He used it to send a short text that contained the address of the hotel.

The recipient was a woman named Tara.

Then, he sat on a park bench a half block from the cheap motel and waited. He felt exposed and had considered wearing the motorcycle helmet he'd tossed into the trash. But that would look bizarre.

No, the odds of someone spotting him now were slim.

Instead of worrying, he calculated the time it would have taken Tara to leave Chicago and get to St. Louis.

She had a slightly shorter trip than his from Oklahoma but he had hit the road immediately.

In his best estimation, she should have been very close by now.

When he'd called her from the Dupree trailer, he'd only told her to start heading for St. Louis, but he hadn't given her an address because he wasn't sure exactly where he would wind up.

Now that she had the address of the cheap hotel, it would only be a short wait.

Still, Stone had seen it all and he had no illusions.

There was always a chance he couldn't trust her.

If she had turned on him, the cops would arrive first. Probably plainclothes. Or maybe even Feds.

If she was still loyal, she would show up alone with no one tailing her.

For now, all he could do was wait.

CHAPTER ELEVEN

"How do you like Chicago?"

Tallon smiled. Pauling always had the strangest openings on phone calls.

He had just finished one of his epic runs through the desert. He'd showered and dressed, but a thin bead of sweat had broken out along his forehead. His legs ached and it would take several hours to recover. Rather than sit down, though, he opted to keep moving and now, he was back outside.

"Chicago's a great town," he said. "Hot dogs, pizza and beer. What's not to love?"

He was standing outside the main building of his adobe ranch, appraising its curb appeal, as the realtors called it. It still bothered him how many

times Connie had referred to his home as "interesting." He chalked most of it up to the fact that
she was twenty years older than him and wasn't
used to the kind of minimalism military guys
liked in their living quarters.

"Why?" he asked.

"An old case of mine from the Bureau has sort
of come back to life and I'm thinking of going to
Chicago to help out."

"The Feds are letting you do that?"

He heard her hesitate. "Not exactly. I may
help someone who was involved. A civilian."

As always, Tallon wondered if the call was
being monitored. He knew Pauling had state-of-
the-art security, just as he did, but you never
knew. When the FBI pulled out all the stops, they
could do just about anything.

"Well, I'm between jobs right now, so the
timing is perfect," he answered. "But it sounds
like you're not sure if you're actually going to
do it."

"I think I'm definitely going to Chicago and
at least meet with my potential client, even if I
don't take the job," Pauling said. "So, we could at
least have a weekend together even if it doesn't
pan out."

Tallon had to admit, he was getting a touch

impatient with their living arrangements. But they were in a weird place. He didn't want to sell his ranch, and Pauling wasn't exactly in a hurry to move out of New York and in with him. So they were in a bit of a purgatory.

Now that he had toyed around with the idea of selling his property and promptly decided against it, the same dynamic was back in play. If they spent time together in Chicago, then what? Would he go back to New York with Pauling? Or would she come back here with him?

"And then after, I thought I would come out to your place for awhile," she said, as if reading his mind.

Immediately, his mood improved.

"Do you want to take care of the flight arrangements to Chicago, or do you want me to?" he asked.

CHAPTER TWELVE

It was a Lake Forest mansion, along the shore of Lake Michigan with a vista that was easily worth a few million dollars. This was the neighborhood of Al Capones and Michael Jordans and tycoons of various industry.

A sprawling yard with a winding driveway leading up to a massive structure three stories tall with multiple wings shooting off the central building. The home was awash in old-world craftsmanship: limestone block, custom wrought iron works, heavy wooden doors.

Brooks had seen it all before. Not this particular home, but many like it. His employers tended to favor the look of old money, even if they'd made their questionable millions in less than a decade.

He was shown to the study by a thick-chested man in a suit tailored to display said torso.

Brooks was always amused by bodybuilders. A passion for lifting heavy objects didn't serve one well in a fight. At least by itself, gymnasium-supplied strength didn't do much on its own. Whenever he saw a huge slab of meat stuffed into an Armani suit trying to intimidate, Brooks always wanted to ask: but do you really know how to fight? With hands? Guns? Knives?

Most of them didn't.

In the library, floor-to-ceiling shelves were filled with leather books. Oil paintings hung on the wall. The faint smell of whiskey and cigar smoke seemed to permeate the heavy wood beams.

Completely not fitting in with the scene before him, a man in a peach-colored suit sat in one of the leather club chairs, a drink in hand. In addition to the glow-in-the-dark suit, the man had multiple gold rings on each hand. He looked a little like Elton John circa the late 90s.

Brooks knew him, of course. His name was Leonard and he was a go-between. He didn't own the house. He was simply allowed access to the mansion in order to hold occasional, sensitive meetings. It was also why he was willing to dress like a flamboyantly gay rock star: his bosses were nowhere near the conversation.

"Ah, Brooks," Leonard said. He smiled, revealing teeth that had seen no small amount of bleach, polish, and veneers. "Care for a drink?"

"No."

Leonard smirked. "Your social graces never cease to impress." Leonard spoke with an affected tone, like he was being filmed for a reality show.

Brooks stood in front of Leonard and waited.

"Please sit."

"No thank you. You called me here for a job. What is it?"

Brooks had dealt with Leonard before and despised the man. Brooks despised the way Leonard loved the sound of his own, mellifluous voice. The man would use fifty words to say something that only required ten.

One of these days, Brooks would assign himself the elimination of Leonard, when he wasn't concerned with the consequences. He would do the job pro bono.

"It's a doozy, my boy," Leonard said, batting his eyelashes. "It seems a certain federal prisoner has flown the coop and no one can find him. There's a dossier on the table with everything you need."

"So the Feds are involved," Brooks said.

"Indeed."

"I hope my fee reflects the degree of difficulty."

"It does. You're not dealing with the B-team here, sunshine."

Brooks picked up the folder and asked, "How soon?"

"As soon as possible. And yes, that is reflected in your fee, too."

The sun was setting over Lake Michigan and a swath of burnt ocher filled the study, turning the wood from dark oak into a honey color.

Brooks headed for the library's exit but Leonard had one more thing to say.

"Be aware failure is not acceptable on this one, Brooksy Boy."

Brooks didn't break stride, simply held his right hand up behind his head with the middle finger extended.

CHAPTER THIRTEEN

Stone Morticelli's former girlfriend was the polar opposite of his ex-wife, which is what had attracted him to her in the first place.

While Veronica was a curvy brunette both intelligent and beautiful, Tara Norcross was a rail-thin bottle blonde with fake boobs and an addictive personality. When Stone had first met her, she was just getting into stripping but already fully immersed in a cocaine addiction. Stone had stepped in, stopped her path from the usual: stripper to escort to street hooker – and set her up in his bachelor pad.

As physically attractive as Tara was, Stone had found her personality endearing. Tara was a dangerous woman, up for anything, and frequently in some kind of trouble. Life with her was never boring, which Stone both loved and hated.

The chemistry between them had been wild and wicked. They'd spent many a hot and sweaty night working between the silk sheets of the king bed in his secret apartment. Of course, he later found out it hadn't been that much of a secret – that Veronica had known all about it.

What's done is done, he thought.

And even though he hadn't seen Tara since he'd been incarcerated and she certainly hadn't written or visited – that wasn't Tara's style –Stone knew she was fiercely loyal and would do anything for him.

He hadn't given her his room number, so he waited from his vantage point, keeping an eye on the front of the cheap hotel, and her car. She had owned a red Porsche and loved it more than anything in the world. He figured she probably still drove it, but people change.

Whatever car Tara arrived in, Stone was confident it wouldn't be ordinary.

He ran the most likely scenario through his mind. Stone knew the man at the front desk wouldn't give her any information, like his room number, namely because he wasn't the one who'd given him his room and it wasn't the kind of place that kept records.

Just as he was beginning to feel the first seeds of doubt take hold, a red Porsche pulled up outside the hotel. A blonde exited the car, paused to confirm the address and then went inside.

Stone left his spot and ducked into the corner convenience store next to the hotel. If he knew Tara, she would get no information from the front desk and then come back out. She would probably debate going back to her car and waiting for Stone to contact her. But first, she would come in to the convenience store for a pack of smokes or some liquor before going back to her car to wait.

As it turned out, Stone himself didn't have long to wait. He was pretending to peruse a shelf of various processed donuts when he heard the door open. Stone could almost sense her presence. He waited and heard a female ask for a half-pint of vodka.

He smiled.

Stone made his way to the door and as she passed him, he said her name.

Tara stopped but didn't turn, instead, looking into her purse as if she couldn't find her keys.

Stone, as always, was impressed by her composure.

"Room 312. Meet me there in five minutes," he said.

She went back to her car and Stone asked the proprietor, a white man with a dirty goatee if there was a bathroom. The guy gestured toward the back of the store. Stone passed the bathroom and found the back door to the place. It opened up onto an alley.

He went down the length of the alley and found the employee's entrance to the hotel. Stone climbed the stairs to the third floor, unlocked his room and waited.

When the door opened a few minutes later Stone took Tara into his arms. She had gained a little weight since he'd last seen her, but it had been in all the right places.

"Hello Stone," she said. Her green eyes danced before his and she kissed him.

"You look great," he said to her. "And I'm not saying that because I just got out of prison."

She laughed and then Stone showed her exactly what he meant.

CHAPTER FOURTEEN

Pauling was the first to arrive at Chicago's O'Hare airport so she picked up her Cadillac rental car and drove around to arrivals to wait for Tallon. His flight would have landed only a half hour after hers but by the time she got the car and came back, she should only have to wait a few minutes.

There weren't too many cops badgering people illegally parked and waiting to pick up their loved ones at baggage claim. Pauling pulled to the side and put the car in park.

While she waited, she took out her cell phone and used an app that allowed her to check on her apartment in New York. Pauling toggled through the various camera angles and was reassured that everything looked normal. She was also able to check the security system to make sure that power had never been cut, and no attempts to disarm the system had been made.

It wasn't that she had any serious thoughts Stone Morticelli would come to New York and try to kill her, but she had, in fact, spent a small fortune on the security system and utilizing it made her feel like she was getting her money's worth.

Not to mention, she'd put away a lot of bad guys during her time with the Bureau and Stone wasn't necessarily the only criminal who harbored ill will toward her.

With that done, she scrolled through some of the documents she had forwarded to herself before she left New York for Chicago. They mostly had to do with Stone Morticelli's arrest and the subsequent trial targeting the legendary head of the Chicago Mob: Vito Barranca Sr.

She also read through the files on Veronica Morticelli, even though she'd already done that on the plane.

A text from Tallon popped up saying he had his bag and was waiting by Door #3. Pauling put the Cadillac in gear and nosed her way up until she saw him.

God he looks good, she thought.

Pauling popped the trunk, got out and met Tallon at the back of the car. They embraced and she kissed him hard. He had a little bit of stubble and it scratched her face, but it felt good. He smelled like he always did; a touch of the outdoors and a very subtle cologne she'd given him as a gift.

He smiled at her.

"Thanks for picking me up," he said. "Want me to drive?"

"Nah, I got it," she replied and got back behind the wheel.

Once she'd navigated through the arrivals traffic and made it out to the freeway, Tallon asked her, "So where to first?"

Pauling had already given him the big picture so she simply said, "Veronica's place is downtown. We'll start there and see what the situation is. If it looks like we're going to help her, then we look for a place close by to stay. I have no intention of moving in with her."

"Good," Tallon said. "Tell me what she's like."

"Smart. Tough. And now it seems, scared."

"This Stone guy would have to be pretty stupid to try to go after her," Tallon pointed out. "You'd think a guy fresh out of prison would do anything to avoid going back. You sure he's even thinking about revenge?"

Pauling maneuvered the Caddy around an SUV that was slightly swerving in its lane. As she passed, she saw the driver trying to text and drive. It always pissed her off.

"If I were putting money down in Vegas, I would bet against it," she answered. "But you never know. I also feel a slight responsibility for Veronica as she was a key player in bringing down her husband. If it makes her feel better to have me around, then I might be willing to do it. I'm glad you could join me," she said and glanced over at him.

He was looking out the window.

"What's the matter?" she asked.

Tallon snapped out of his reverie. "Nothing, just thinking about how unpredictable human beings can be."

"Such as?"

"Breaking out of prison in this day and age is something someone does who has no options," he said. "I mean, everyone has cell phones and internet connections. It's so hard for fugitives to stay hidden. For him to break out, there has to be a reason. A goal. A motivation."

"And you're saying killing his wife in a fit of revenge isn't one of those?"

Tallon turned his attention from the window back to her.

"No," he said. "I'm just saying if that's not his goal, then what is?"

CHAPTER FIFTEEN

It isn't easy to find a parking spot in Chicago for surveillance, as the two men in the dark blue Crown Vic could attest. They'd circled the block of the luxury high-rise four times before they finally spotted a guy in a suit with a briefcase pulling a four-door Porsche out of a space.

"What's the point of that?" the guy in the front passenger seat said. His name was Talbert and he had orange-ish hair and a weak, nearly translucent moustache. "A four-door Porsche? That's like riding a Harley while wearing a diaper."

The driver, a man known only to his associates as Bear, ignored the comment. He hated Talbert and wanted to punch him so hard the orange sherbet moustache would fall off the obnoxious man's face.

Bear felt like it was being trapped in a car with a bad version of Seinfeld: Ever notice (insert trivial item here) and then say, *what's up with that?* Or, in the case of the Porsche comment, try to make some half-ass comparison.

Bear, called that because he was six-and-a half-feet tall and weighed close to three hundred and fifty pounds, wanted to ask the boss if he could be teamed with anyone but Talbert. The problem was, you had to be very careful about asking that kind of thing.

If it was taken the wrong way and you were seen as anything but a "team player," you could find yourself on the bottom of Lake Michigan with your five-hundred-dollar Italian leather shoes encased in concrete.

"Let's focus on looking for that whack job Morticelli," Bear said.

"Stone," Talbert said. "How would you like to be called that all the time? It's like that saying, 'dumb as a box of rocks.' Man, someone started calling me Stone, I'd beat them until they started calling me Daddy."

Bear rolled his eyes behind his dark sunglasses.

This was a fool's errand anyway, he thought. No way Stone Morticelli was coming to knock off his ex-wife after escaping from prison. Bear had never met the man, but he'd heard he was no idiot, despite the nickname.

No, this luxurious building – Bear had heard apartments started at north of two mill – was home to people like the couple getting out of the Cadillac and tossing the keys to the valet.

The woman was a total hottie, a little older than Bear liked, but she had sandy-colored hair with maybe some blonde highlights, and a killer body. The guy was maybe her security guard or boyfriend. He was built, moved like an athlete. Bear thought he might be ex-military just by the way he carried himself.

No, Stone wouldn't show up here, Bear thought.

It'd be fancy pants couples like those two.

CHAPTER SIXTEEN

"Did you see the two guys in the Crown Vic?" Tallon asked.

"Sure did," Pauling replied as they walked from the Cadillac they'd just turned over to the valet, toward the high-rise where Veronica lived.

The Chicago air was crisp and cool. It felt almost dense to Tallon after being out West for the past few weeks. Now, he was in a concrete canyon as they said. Huge buildings towered over everyone, casting the streets in shadow, the wind funneled between them, accelerating into a man-made battering ram.

People walked with their shoulders hunched forward, as if they were expecting someone or something to clobber them from behind.

Tallon didn't have anything against cities per se, in fact, he often had a helluva good time when he was in one, but for daily living he preferred the wide open spaces.

Take the two hoods in the Crown Vic. They were either cops, detectives, private security or thugs. Maybe a combination of all four. Tallon wondered if they were here to provide security for the former Mrs. Morticelli, but discarded the idea. They didn't look like Feebies. He knew hired muscle when he saw it and that was his best guess on the guys in the Crown Vic.

Tallon followed Pauling inside and let her handle the information desk. Soon, they each had a visitor pass and were taking the elevator to the penthouse floor.

The doors opened and they entered a marble foyer with white leather and steel couches encircling a set of large, wooden French doors.

Two armed guards stood outside the doors.

Clearly, they had been watching them via video and monitoring their arrival because one of them turned and opened the doors.

Revealed in the doorway was a woman who reminded Tallon of a young Raquel Welch.

She had wavy brown hair, beautiful dark eyes and a body full of curves and wicked promises.

Whew, Tallon thought. Talk about a presence.

"Good to see you again, Lauren," the woman said. Her voice was as smooth and silky as her curves.

"You too, Victoria," Pauling replied. She turned to Tallon. "This is my partner, Michael Tallon."

Tallon shook Victoria's hand, surprised by the strength of her grip. She had an expression of curiosity and, he thought, a slight amusement. As if she'd been able to read his thoughts.

"Come inside please," Victoria said.

They followed her and Tallon couldn't help but notice the way she walked. The gentle sway of her hips was like an invitation, and he forced himself to stop thinking about Pauling's client that way. He was here on business.

The apartment was monstrous – at least ten thousand square feet, if not more. There were floor-to-ceiling windows around the perimeter, offering views of the Chicago skyline and on one side, Lake Michigan.

Another pair of security guards flanked each end of the cavernous space.

What does she need us for? Tallon thought.

"Coffee?" Veronica asked.

"No thank you," Pauling replied. They followed Veronica to a seating area composed of a loveseat and two chairs. Veronica took the center of the love seat and Tallon and Pauling each took a chair.

Tallon thought it was one of the most comfortable chairs he'd ever sat in, and it faced Lake Michigan – a beautiful sheet of blue-green glass. He wished he had a beer and could sit and wait for dusk.

"Thank you for coming," Veronica said. Her voice was like butter, but Tallon loved Pauling's, which sounded like a jazz singer after a midnight performance that included whiskey and cigarettes.

"My first thought is why do you need us?" Pauling said, gesturing toward the security personnel arrayed in the apartment. "And I'm sure you have more than what I'm seeing here."

"Yes, there's a small office that houses the apartment's security system," Veronica said. "It's being monitored as we speak and there are more personnel outside the building. All told, I have a team of about twelve. Three times the normal number."

"Your husband would have to be suicidal to try to attack this place," Tallon said. "And he would be unsuccessful even if that was his state of mind."

Veronica smiled at Tallon, and he had to physically exert himself to stay focused.

Jesus, get a grip, he thought.

"I have to be honest," Veronica said. "I asked you to come here under false pretenses."

Tallon heard Pauling sigh and when he glanced at her, she had an expression of annoyance.

"You're not afraid he's coming here to kill you," Pauling said.

"No, I'm not."

"Then why did you say you were?"

"Because you're one of, if not the best, private investigators in the country. Maybe the world," Veronica said. "I've got tabs on you, Lauren. I know all about your exploits. I even know some of Mr. Tallon's stories as well."

Tallon wasn't falling for the flattery.

"So..." he said.

"So I don't think Stone is coming to kill me. But I do think he's going to kill someone. In fact, he's already killed three people. No, my reason for bringing you here is because I want you to help me answer a simple question."

"And what would that be?" Pauling asked.

"Why?"

"Why what?" Tallon asked.

"Why did my ex-husband, a very intelligent, powerful and dangerous man, even behind bars, go berserk and kill three people?"

"Incarceration does strange things to people," Pauling pointed out. "Dehumanizes them. Transforms them into something they perhaps were not."

"Not Michael. Not my husband. He was called Stone for a reason. That was his personality. His character. His will. Like goddamned granite."

"I'm confused," Tallon said.

Veronica crossed one of her shapely legs, put her hand on the leather couch. Tallon noticed the symmetry of her fingers, the shapeliness of her arm.

"I believe someone tried to kill my husband in prison and he acted in self-defense," Veronica explained. "I want to know who ordered him killed and I want to know why."

Pauling shook her head. "Are you kidding me?" she asked. "He's in the Mafia. They kill each other all the time. Sometimes for no reason."

"I don't think that was the case this time," she said. "He kept his mouth shut. He was doing his time. There would have been no reason to kill him."

"Prisons are dangerous places," Tallon added. "You think there has to be a reason for violence? Try boredom. Fun. Guys kill each other in the slammer for a pack of cigarettes."

"That's maximum security. Stone was in medium security. A federal prison. Not exactly death row, if you know what I mean," Veronica countered.

A yacht crossed Lake Michigan on the distant horizon and Tallon tried to figure out where he might be going. North. Probably toward Milwaukee.

"My turn to ask a question," Pauling said "What do you care? You testified against him. You had a hand in locking him up."

"We both know I had no choice. Stone knows that, too."

She tilted her head toward the windows and the light fell across her impeccable jawline.

"Despite our troubled history, I still love him and I know, deep down, he still loves me."

Veronica turned and focused her dark eyes on Pauling. They were burning with an intensity that surprised Tallon.

"I want you to find the scum who tried to kill my husband."

"I'm not with the FBI anymore," Pauling said. "I can't arrest them."

She smiled again, but it was different. This one gave Tallon a nearly imperceptible chill.

"I know," she said.

CHAPTER SEVENTEEN

Brooks was a bit surprised by the carelessness on display. Stone Morticelli certainly should have suspected that someone would have put a tail on his ex-girlfriend Tara Norcross. Even worse, she was a bottle blonde who drove a red Porsche. She was practically impossible to miss.

Amateurs, Brooks thought.

He'd simply sped down from Chicago to St. Louis when the GPS tracker placed on Tara's car by Brooks's employers had started pinging its way out of the Windy City.

Brooks had arrived only thirty minutes after her and at that point, she'd been parked outside a cheap hotel.

Beyond the hotel was a section of abandoned

city blocks which provided plenty of free parking without cameras. East Saint Louis was a very easy place to work if you wanted to avoid the cops. On the other hand, someone trying to steal his car, a new-ish Ford SUV, was a very real possibility.

However, this job wouldn't take very long, Brooks thought. Stone, being fresh out of prison, was probably banging away at the first woman he'd touched in several years.

Still in the SUV, Brooks withdrew his weapon of choice, a Beretta 9mm with a threaded barrel. He twisted on a sound suppressor and made sure he had an extra magazine in his pocket, not that he would need it. He figured two shots into each of them and he'd be done.

From an inner pocket of his suit coat, he withdrew a small gold vial. He popped off the cap and inhaled a snort of cocaine. He always liked to have an edge when he did a job. It intensified the rush.

Brooks exited the vehicle, locked it, and approached the hotel.

CHAPTER EIGHTEEN

How embarrassing, Stone thought. He felt like a teenager after his first backseat adventure, the whole thing over in about three minutes.

He was out of practice, he rationalized. His only female company in prison had been the occasional vintage copy of Playboy secretly passed around by the inmates. Who could blame him for not having the stamina he once had? Especially with a woman like Tara?

In the bathroom, he splashed cold water on his face. He knew he'd be ready to go in a very short amount of time, and that the next session would last a lot longer.

I'll get better with practice, he thought.

Stone smiled at the thought of Tara driving all this way for...that. Well, it wasn't the only reason she was here. He needed help and she was the only one—

Pfft.

Pfft.

A sound suppressor despite its name, makes noise. In a quiet hotel room, the sound actually carries quite well.

Stone's hands froze in mid-air. He knew what one sounded like. He'd used them many times during his professional career.

Now, he knew exactly what had happened. Someone had followed Tara here from Chicago. Despite the fact Stone had observed her and spotted no one. Which meant there was a tracking device on the Porsche, most certainly.

And Tara was dead.

Fury rose within him but he wasn't about to attack a guy with a gun. Probably an enforcer who knew how to use it.

Footsteps outside the bathroom door.

The Porsche.

Stone had no choice. He'd left both guns on the night table next to the bed. They were no good to him now.

He turned to the square window with privacy

glass and slid it upward, praying it wasn't painted shut.

It opened noiselessly. Probably for people who wanted to smoke in the bathroom or run from the cops. He'd chosen the right hotel, after all.

Stone slid through the opening. Dressed only in a pair of underwear, he felt the cold steel of the fire escape on his bare feet. He went down the escape noiselessly. Behind him, he heard a sound.

Pfft.

Followed by wood splintering.

Pfft.

He hit the sidewalk running and rounded the building just as a bullet exploded next to his head. It hit the edge of the brick building's wall and fragments stung his face.

Stone ran for the Porsche, praying that Tara hadn't changed. She never carried her car keys with her, but kept them in the concealed sunglasses compartment. Her reasoning? No one would be stupid enough to leave a Porsche unlocked with the keys inside.

He wrenched open the door, sure a bullet was about to smack him between the shoulder blades at any second, and opened the sunglasses compartment.

The keys fell out.

He jammed them into the ignition, fired the car up and threw it into gear. He fishtailed onto the street and took the first left turn.

Getting away wasn't his priority.

His first order of business was to find that goddamned GPS tracker.

And then he would find out who was behind all this and who killed Tara.

Stone opened his enormous hands, flexed them, felt the strength within.

He would find them, make them pay.

And pay dearly.

CHAPTER NINETEEN

"I think I need some more background," Tallon said. "Because her story stinks."

"I agree," Pauling said.

They had booked a suite in the ultra luxurious Four Seasons Hotel. Namely because it was within a stone's throw of Veronica's apartment building.

They valeted the car again, checked in, and rode the elevator to the room. It was nice and spacious, but a fraction of the size of Veronica's place. The view was nice, too. A sliver of Lake Michigan, and plenty of Chicago skyline.

Tallon grabbed a beer from the mini fridge and a small bottle of wine. He poured Pauling a glass.

She started with an overview of the case and

then said, "So Stone Morticelli was a medium-sized fish in the whole FBI operation. The real prize was a man named Vito Barranca Sr."

"I've heard of him," Tallon said. "He's dead now, right?"

"Yep, gunned down in front of a martini bar before we could put him away."

"Convenient."

"Yeah," Pauling said. "In a way, the FBI was satisfied because Barranca was gone. The old man was a real bastard, smug, too. So while there was frustration we didn't bring down his whole operation, he was certainly killed because of our impending case."

"How does Stone Morticelli fit in?"

"Stone kept his mouth shut, and so did most of the others involved, but all of the really good stuff was aimed for Barranca. Murder. Murder-for-hire, etc. So we had to settle for busting Morticelli on mostly conspiracy charges."

Tallon shrugged his shoulders. "A bad guy off the street. A few in prison, not bad for a day's work."

"Yeah, but Stone's attorney was this guy named Peter Kleinfeld, the most notorious Mob lawyer in Chicago. Not only is the guy scum, but he's pretty damned good at what he does. So it made matters worse, for sure. Plus, the Cook County prosecutors dragged their feet on a few things."

"What about the attorney general?"

"The Bureau had just taken one of the biggest budget cuts in its existence. With Barranca dead, it was decided to let Chicago handle the case. If the old man had been alive, it would have been different."

"So someone was on the take?"

Now it was Pauling's turn to shrug. "It's Chicago. Nothing would surprise me."

Tallon leaned back and stretched.

"Who killed Barranca?" he asked. "A rival?"

"No one knows for sure," Pauling said. "Most of us at the time believed it was one of his own."

"You mean, one of the men in his crew?"

"No, one of his own in the truest sense."

Tallon suddenly realized what she meant.

"His son," she said. "Vito Barranca Jr."

CHAPTER TWENTY

"I swear to God, Vito, there was no way we could have known."

Bear and Talbert stood before the man they sometimes referred to as 'Junior' but only behind his back and only when they knew there were absolutely no listening devices anywhere that could be used against them.

They weren't worried about listening devices laced by the authorities. They were worried about their own. Vito had already murdered at least two people who had dared to call him Junior to his face. You only called him Junior when you were absolutely positive it couldn't get back to him.

"Veronica went and hired two private investigators," Vito said. He was a big man, not as big as Bear, but he had a bull neck and broad shoulders.

His face was narrow and he had a large, hawkish nose. "You saw them go in and come out, and you didn't think to follow them?"

Bear knew there was no way they could have known the couple had gone in to meet with Veronica, and he suspected Vito knew it too. This was simply a case of the boss blowing off steam.

"I really thought they looked like a couple," Talbert said.

Uh-oh, here it comes, Bear thought.

"I mean, what's up with that?" Talbert continued. "A private investigator team posing as a couple? What a joke."

They were in the back office of the private club from which Vito operated his empire. It was the same place his father had established over five decades ago.

Vito looked at Talbert like he was deciding whether to punch him in the face or the gut.

Just then, the door to the main room opened.

"Boss?"

Vito's right-hand man, Johnny Knocks, stuck his head between the door and jamb. He had an impressive head of silver and black hair, and liked to wear flashy suits. He also had a strange habit of knocking his knuckles on the table before or after he made a statement. Hence, Johnny Knocks.

"News from St. Louis," he said.

"What the hell do I care about St. Louis?"

"This you might," Johnny Knocks said, absentmindedly giving the door two additional knocks. "It's about Stone."

"Shit," Vito said.

"Yeah, someone tried to take him out. Killed his girlfriend – that chick named Tara."

"Too bad, she was a sweet piece of ass," Vito said, his eyes cloudy with emotion suddenly.

"Stone survived?" Bear asked.

"Supposedly," Johnny Knocks said. "Rumor is he ran out of some fleabag hotel in his boxers and took off in a Porsche."

"The man always had style, I'll say that," Vito said. "Who told you all this?"

"You remember Paulie? Owns the market a block from the stadium?"

Vito nodded.

"Boss, I know this sounds like a stupid question, but I thought we were going to kill Morticelli," Talbert said. Bear winced at how dumb his 'partner' sounded. "Sounds like we got competition."

Vito took out a cigar, nipped off the end, fired it up and blew smoke at the ceiling.

"Yeah, that's the bad news," Johnny Knocks said.

Vito rolled his eyes. "Spit it out for Christ's sake."

"Rumor is a guy in a really nice suit came out of the hotel after Stone," Johnny said. He sat down at the table next to Bear, gave its surface a quick double tap with his knuckles. "Guy had on like a double-breasted number with pinstripes. Looked really sharp, I guess.'

"Oh no," Vito said.

Talbert looked at Bear, confused.

Bear said the name softly, under his breath.

"Brooks."

CHAPTER TWENTY-ONE

The State's Attorney for Cook County is the second largest prosecuting office in the country with over eight hundred attorneys and nearly two thousand employees.

At the very top was a woman named Mary Chang.

Ms. Chang, or "Let 'em Hang Chang," was not in her office. Nor was she in her million-dollar townhouse just north of the city. Instead, she was in the arms of one of the most successful, infamous and highest-paid defense attorneys in Chicago. His name was Peter Kleinfeld.

They made an interesting couple. Mary Chang was slim, with a sharp face, luxurious black hair and a killer smile.

Kleinfeld had a receding hairline with bushy hair that made him look like a circus clown. He had a thick nose and wore dark glasses. He was barely 5' 7" with small feet and hands.

There was nothing physically impressive about Peter Kleinfeld.

His mind, on the other hand, was beyond exceptional. He'd made a fortune defending some of the most notorious clients in the world.

One of them, Michael "Stone" Morticelli, was now a free man. However, he did not have Peter Kleinfeld to thank for that.

"When did you hear?" Chang asked him.

They were in Chang's brownstone just north of the city. A year ago, she had paid over two million dollars for it, although that amount was never listed on any public records. Her lover had made sure of that.

Chang traced her finger along Kleinfeld's bare chest. It was hairless, and he had the beginning of a small pair of man boobs.

"Right away, of course," he said. "A man in my profession with my clients hears immediately when a former mobster escapes federal prison."

"So what are you doing about it?" she asked.

"Not make the same mistake twice," Kleinfeld said.

"Who? How?"

"I've already got a man on the job," he said. "You'd like him."

"Why's that?"

"He's a very sharp dresser."

CHAPTER TWENTY-TWO

With the Ford SUV fired up, Brooks was able to turn on the GPS tracking screen that looked like an iPad on steroids. He waited, like a sniper zeroing in on his target, until finally the red circle with its black border appeared on the freeway outside East Saint Louis, heading west toward Kansas City.

It made sense to Brooks. Stone wasn't about to go running back to Chicago, and he certainly wouldn't head south back toward Oklahoma.

No, going west was the right decision.

Or maybe east.

Brooks wondered if Morticelli had too many enemies on the East Coast in places like New York, Jersey and Philly.

Probably.

Which made the west more attractive.

Stone could hide out in KC and then either veer south toward Vegas and Los Angeles, or north toward Seattle, even Vancouver. He'd have to be really prepared to cross into Canada, though. Fresh out of prison he certainly didn't have a passport. Maybe he could bribe someone.

Brooks put the Ford in gear and quickly maneuvered his way out of the downtrodden community and launched himself into the fast lane on the freeway. He soon had the big vehicle doing ninety-five miles per hour as he eased in and out of slower-moving drivers.

As he drove, he thought back to the scene in the hotel room. It had been a shame to kill the girl but once he'd gotten the door to the room open, her eyes had gone wide and when she opened her mouth, he knew it was to yell out to Stone, who was probably in the bathroom.

He'd shot her in the forehead before she could make a sound. But a silencer on a pistol still makes a noise and goddamned Morticelli must have heard it. There were two pistols on the table by the bed so Brooks had known Morticelli probably wasn't armed.

But by the time he shot out the lock on the bathroom door, Stone was gone.

Bad luck.

Brooks wasn't worried. He was a professional after all and sometimes he knew you had to flush the game from their hiding spots before you could shoot them out of the sky.

Now, he raced ahead and was surprised at how fast he was catching up to Stone. He was driving a Porsche, but must have been concerned with the cops and wasn't willing to break the speed limit.

Perfect, Brooks thought. *Because I'm happy to risk it.*

He sped ahead and within fifteen minutes was right behind the red dot on the tracking screen.

Brooks found himself looking at a rented RV – he knew it was rented because it had a big sign on the back that read RentAnRV.com with a goofy picture of a couple and a moose. He maneuvered the SUV around the truck and shot forward, only to glance back at the tracker screen and see with dismay that the red dot was now behind him.

He slowed down and pulled up next to the RV. It was possible Stone was inside, but more likely that he'd found the GPS bug and slapped it on the RV.

Still, his employers would want to know one way or the other. No loose ends. He thought back to what Leonard had said: *failure is not acceptable.*

Brooks rolled the window down and shot out both tires on the right side of the lumbering vehicle.

It swerved erratically and he watched as it pulled to the side of the road.

He drove up behind it.

A door opened and a man with a Green Bay Packers t-shirt stepped out. He had a beer belly and his face was flushed red.

He looked at Brooks.

"What the heck happened?" he said. "Two flat tires? How did that happen?"

He looked at the tires and then back up at Brooks. He seemed puzzled. "How am I supposed to change these tires? I doubt I have two spares."

Brooks walked forward.

The man in the Packers shirt glanced back up at Brooks. It seemed to dawn on him that the strange man in the nice suit hadn't offered to help, hadn't given a reason as to why he'd stopped.

"Hey–" the man said, suddenly realizing that the stranger might have had something to do with his predicament.

Brooks shot him in the heart.

The chubby man toppled to the side of the road just as a woman stepped out. She had a bad perm haircut from the 80s and a Wisconsin Badger t-shirt. She looked down at her husband, confused, then back up at Brooks, her face a mixture of shock and fear, her mouth forming an "o."

Brooks shot her before she could say anything. She slumped back against the door to the RV and slid underneath, a streak of blood smeared the white aluminum.

Brooks stepped over her dead body and boarded the RV, the gun in front of him.

There was a bag of potato chips and a bowl of dip on the center table. In the back, an unmade bed. The only other space was a door that must have led to the bathroom.

He doubted Stone Morticelli could even fit in the space, but he might.

Failure is not acceptable.

Brooks stepped up and fired six shots through the door at varying heights.

He heard a bump from inside and carefully opened the door.

An old woman wearing jeans around her ankles and a Wisconsin Dells sweatshirt fell out onto the floor, bleeding from multiple places. In her hands was an issue of Vogue with Rihanna on the cover.

Brooks left the RV and went around back. He searched until he found the tracker bug – placed just behind the license plate of the RV.

He smiled.

Stone might not be so stupid after all.

CHAPTER TWENTY-THREE

S tone wondered if the owners of the rental RV were going to be okay, but he had a feeling they weren't.

At the same time, he wasn't going to worry about them. Bad things happen to innocent people all the time. And who really knew if someone was innocent? Maybe they cheated on their taxes, or poisoned the neighbor's dog.

He wasn't saying they deserved to die, but in his opinion there weren't any angels anymore in this day and age.

Stone knew he had only a limited time to make a play and that had to be now. He was still in the Porsche, making a beeline for Chicago. It felt strange driving Tara's car. He realized less than a few hours ago she was sitting in the exact same seat, headed to St. Louis out of blind allegiance to a man she hadn't seen in two years.

Bad things happen to good people sometimes.

When he'd stuck the GPS tracker to the back of the RV, he'd done so at a rest stop in southern Illinois. Since he'd seen the couple and an older woman go into the convenience store/fast food plaza, Stone, still wearing only a pair of boxers, had slipped into the RV and grabbed a pair of shorts, sneakers and a Milwaukee Bucks t-shirt.

The shorts were a little big and the sneakers a touch small, but at least he looked semi-normal.

Inside a compartment between the front driver's seat and passenger seat, he found a cell phone. It was turned off and he assumed it was either little used or for emergency purposes only.

Well, he considered this an emergency.

Back in the Porsche, he gunned it straight toward Chicago. However, rather than going the fastest approach – straight up I-55 – he'd cut over east and caught I-57, just in case the cops had already put out information on the Porsche.

This was no time to screw around, though, and he pushed the German sports car well over 100 mph when he was confident there weren't any speed traps ahead.

As he drove, his mind worked.

He had been certain that Vito Barranca had put the hit on him in prison. Stone knew Junior blamed him for his father's death. But Stone had figured by honoring the code and keeping his mouth shut, the other members of the Syndicate would not allow Junior to make the contract.

At first, he figured Junior had simply gone rogue.

Now, he wasn't so sure.

The hit in the hotel, the killing of Tara, was not the Mob's style.

Stone began to think about his trial, about what he knew, and he was rapidly revising his thoughts on who had sent the Corsican brothers into the showers with shivs.

Stone thought about his attorney, Peter Kleinfeld. The guy was supposed to be the Mob's secret weapon, but the prick hadn't done much to help Stone. Secretly, he was convinced Kleinfeld was the one who'd arranged to have Vito Barranca Sr. murdered outside the martini bar.

There had been something weird between Kleinfeld and the DA at the time, the Asian chick, Mary Chang. Rumors they were making deals on the side for the highest bidders.

Stone had no way of knowing, but as he

neared Chicago, the idea of Junior being the mastermind of his assassination attempt had faded further and further from the realm of possibility.

That left Kleinfeld, or someone else, like his ex-wife.

Veronica had testified against him, after all. She had found out about Tara. And despite that he knew on some level she still loved him. And he felt the same way. But women can be very dangerous and Veronica was a supremely intelligent woman. She could have waited, bided her time, and then put a bounty on his head. To pay him back for cheating on her. For disrespecting her.

He was royally pissed at himself. He should have been more gentle with the prison guard. A good attorney could have argued he killed the Corsicans in self-defense, but no way they were going to let the prison guard's murder go unpunished. Hell, he might have been a candidate for Death Row but Illinois no longer had the death penalty.

Still, life without parole wasn't much better.

Stone powered on the stolen cell phone and punched in a phone number from memory.

He heard the voice on the other end of the line.

"Hello Veronica," he said.

CHAPTER TWENTY-FOUR

P auling had spread out some key documents from her case file on Stone Morticelli. She carried all of her material – even the classified stuff – on her laptop. It was encrypted and placed in "invisible" folders on her hard drive, but she knew where everything was and how to access it quickly.

She'd ordered a printer from the front desk and the Four Seasons, priding themselves on exemplary customer service, had promptly commandeered one, probably from the hotel's Business Center, and it was now in her room.

One of the most important documents she'd printed off was a classic spider web chart of the players in the case against Vito Barranca Sr. and how they related to each other. At one point, in the FBI war room during the Barranca investigation, the spider web chart had been blown up to eight feet high and ten feet wide, taped to an entire wall. They'd spent hundreds of hours staring at it, modifying the relationships, and crossing people off the list on more than one occasion.

"It's amazing to me how small this Stone guy's role was," Tallon said. "If he was so relatively unimportant back then, why all of this and why now?"

"That's a great question," Pauling said. "What it tells me is that we either missed something important or made a mistake. I don't think we screwed up, but it's possible there was a player who we never uncovered."

"And for some reason, that player now decided to pop up and wreak havoc?" Tallon's voice was skeptical.

"It's possible. Strange, but not totally unheard of–"

A knock on the door stopped her in mid-sentence. They hadn't ordered room service and had asked the cleaning staff to hold off on servicing the suite.

Tallon had a pistol in his hand and he walked to the door, standing off to the side.

"Who is it?" Tallon called out.

"Agent Helm, with the FBI. I'm here to see Lauren Pauling, is she there?"

Tallon glanced back at Pauling, who nodded.

Tallon cracked the door and asked for Helm's ID, which he was handed. Satisfied, Tallon handed it back, opened the door and Helm stepped inside.

Behind him, another agent waited.

Helm didn't invite him in and instead, shut the door.

Pauling crossed the room and stood in front of the table which held the documents from Barranca's case.

"How can I help you, Agent Helm?" she asked.

"A heads-up you were coming to Chicago would have been nice," he said. There was a high degree of snark in his tone of voice. "The Bureau took the trouble to warn you back in New York and you don't keep us in the loop?"

"What loop?" she asked.

"We know you visited with Veronica Morticelli."

"Her name's Grasso now. She's a private citizen."

"That's not the point and you know it."

"So what is?"

Helm let out an exasperated sigh. "Come on, let's cut the bullshit. Whatever you're doing here, please don't get in our way. We've got to find Morticelli and get him back in prison before he kills someone else."

"Why *did* he break out and kill someone? Have you found a motive?" Pauling shot back.

"I'm not at liberty to discuss the case," Helm said, sounding like an FBI spokesperson at a press conference. "As I said, don't interfere with our operation here, unless you have new information to share on Stone's whereabouts."

He stopped and waited.

Pauling said nothing.

"Okay, then," Helm replied.

Tallon showed him out and Pauling turned and went back to the table.

"Maybe you didn't miss anything during the investigation and subsequent trial," Tallon offered. "But what about afterward? There must have been some kind of fallout. Did you follow it?" Tallon asked.

"No, I was sort of on loan from New York," she replied. "Budget cuts, remember?"

"Yeah."

"The minute we turned the case over, I said

goodbye to the team, and Veronica, and came back to New York," Pauling said. "And then I had the worst case of my career and before anyone knew it, most of all me, I was out of the Bureau."

Tallon didn't have an answer to that. He looked at the chart on the table.

"The case dragged through the courts forever," Pauling continued, following Tallon's gaze to the chart. "And Stone filed appeals and then he finally got sent to the lockup in Oklahoma."

"So we don't really know about afterward then," Tallon said, pushing forward. "Anything strange happen with the players? I mean, we know Barranca Sr. was gunned down. Vito Jr. took control. What else?"

Pauling was staring at the table.

"Now that you mention it, a few things did happen."

She reached out and tapped the photo of Mary Chang. "She was immediately promoted to State Attorney. Practically the third or fourth most powerful person in Chicago."

Tallon said, "What else?"

"Someone tried to kill Peter Kleinfeld – probably for not getting Barranca Sr. off the hook before he was assassinated."

"That would had to have been sanctioned by the families," Tallon said.

"Yes," Pauling confirmed. "And it would have been Vito Jr. in charge."

"How'd they try to kill him?"

"Car bomb. Killed his driver, but not Kleinfeld. After that, he pretty much went into hiding."

"Or maybe he nursed his wounds and plotted his revenge," Tallon pointed out.

Pauling nodded. "Maybe."

Her phone rang and she glanced at the caller ID.

She picked it up and answered.

"Hello Veronica," she said.

Pauling listened. "When and where?" She scratched down something on a Four Seasons notepad and said, "Okay, got it."

Tallon raised an eyebrow at her.

"Stone wants to meet me," she said. "Turn himself in."

CHAPTER TWENTY-FIVE

Just in time, Stone thought.

He'd pulled into a parking space across from an Irish pub he'd used occasionally as a meeting place back in his glory days.

It was owned by the Irish mob and swept regularly for bugs which made it a popular meeting spot for wiseguys of all ethnicities.

Stone had already exited the Porsche, and now sat a half block away in a bus shelter pretending to study the routes displayed on its outer wall. He was the only person in the shelter and he was worried about how he looked; the wind possessed a chill and he was dressed in shorts and a T-shirt.

He had a plan though, and he was sticking to it.

Stone was on the verge of feeling satisfied when a Chicago PD cruiser drove by. It passed the Porsche and Stone breathed a sigh of relief.

And then the cop's brake lights glowed bright red. The cruiser came to a stop. White lights flashed and the cruiser backed up just behind the Porsche and stopped.

Stone immediately knew a nationwide APB had been put out in full force, all the way from St. Louis. Special alerts had probably been sent to Chicago, too. Maybe even with suggestions to alert patrols around any known Mafia hangouts.

Just as well, he thought. He got to his feet and walked away, turning a corner and disappearing from the cop's view.

Stone walked quickly but somehow looked as if he was in no hurry at all.

He smiled thinking about Lauren Pauling again. Veronica had mentioned the FBI agent's name. He'd always thought Pauling was super hot. Stone had almost forgotten about the woman Fed. She hadn't really been the problem back then.

No, that was someone else.

Stone had always fantasized about meeting Pauling again. Figuring one day he might talk to her. Or sleep with her. Or kill her. Or, best of all, a combination of all three.

CHAPTER TWENTY-SIX

"What the hell do they say he's wearing?" Talbert asked. "A Milwaukee Bucks shirt? What's up with that?"

Bear rolled his eyes and resisted the urge to slap his partner across the face.

"Desperate times, I guess," Bear replied, keeping his voice even with monumental effort.

"He should be a Bulls fan for God's sake," Talbert continued, oblivious to the state of his audience. "What is he, a closet cheesehead?"

Bear turned in his seat. "Talbert, I really need you to shut up and focus on the job at hand. Who cares what he's supposedly wearing? All that matters is if we see a guy fitting that description, we make him go away. End of story. No need to overthink this."

"Remind me what we're supposed to do," Talbert said, rubbing his forehead like he was suffering from information overload.

"He arranged a meet with that couple," Bear said, his patience hanging by a thread. "We're supposed to take care of business, got it?"

"Okay, let's rock 'n' roll," Talbert said.

Bear shook his head. He wasn't sure what he would have preferred: bad comedic observations, or outright clichés.

They both exited the Crown Vic and walked toward the pedestrian underpass not far from Navy pier. It was where supposedly Stone Morticelli was going to turn himself over to that ex-FBI chick and her partner.

At least, that's what Vito said. And when the boss talks, you follow orders, it's that simple, Bear reasoned. He looked around the place. It was a good place for a meet. The weather was cold and threatening rain. No one would be around.

And there'd be no chance of Chicago PD spotting Morticelli and ruining the gig as the whole thing would be practically underground. He looked up into the corners near the entrance.

No cameras, either.

Perfect.

Bear felt the weight of his pistol inside his suit coat. It was a good gun – a Heckler & Koch machine gun that held thirty rounds. Considering his enormous frame, it was easy to carry a gun of this size concealed.

Bear knew Talbert had a pair of .45 automatics, each with high-capacity magazines amounting to around thirty rounds himself.

They walked slowly toward the middle of the tunnel as two people appeared at the other end.

The two groups walked toward each other.

Bear studied them and saw it was a man and a woman. Neither one was wearing a Milwaukee Bucks shirt.

But that was okay, Bear knew.

Because Stone Morticelli wasn't the target.

The man and the woman were.

Michael Tallon.

And Lauren Pauling.

Junior had given Bear and Talbert photos of the two and now, they compared the faces of the couple approaching them.

It was a match.

Bear eased the machine gun from his coat and Talbert did the same.

He didn't know what Junior had against these

people but the orders were to put them down quickly and as quietly as possible. And get out fast.

No problem, Bear thought.

Thirty yards away, the man stopped.

Bear brought up the machine gun and in his peripheral vision, he saw Talbert raise his pistols.

CHAPTER TWENTY-SEVEN

Tallon knew it was wrong the minute the two men entered the tunnel.

He also immediately knew they'd been set up.

Stone Morticelli was most definitely not meeting them. Instead, it was the hired muscle from the Crown Vic. Tallon recognized the bulk of the one, and the weird orange hair and moustache on the other one.

It was a horrible place for a shootout. A tunnel. Plenty of room for ricochets, no place to take cover. Whomever had arranged this must have figured they were going to get the drop.

Something also told Tallon the big man at the other end of the tunnel was carrying some serious firepower.

"Head shots," Tallon said to Pauling.

In a smooth, unhurried motion Tallon drew his 9mm from the holster clipped to his waist and and fired without really aiming. There simply wasn't time to put the sights on target so he shot reflexively, firing five rounds at the big man's head.

It was a type of shooting he'd spent years practicing for a moment just like this. Even as he fired, he hoped Pauling was doing the same thing.

Next to him, he saw Pauling firing.

The two men's weapons erupted in fire from the other end of the tunnel, but the big man fell back, the muzzle of his gun sparking and tearing chunks of cement from the coved ceiling. He crashed to the ground moments before his partner did the same, after barely getting his pistol out and firing one shot into the ground.

Pauling and Tallon cautiously walked forward, their guns still leveled at the men on the ground. The shots had echoed tremendously in the tunnel and the smell of spent ammunition filled the air. Tallon knew they didn't have much time. Someone had to have heard the shots.

They studied the bodies, or more accurately, what was left of them.

Tallon's shots had gone high, blowing off the top of the big man's head.

Pauling's shots had gone low, plowing into her man's chin and ripping the lower half of his face apart.

"Mine fell first," Tallon said, a slight smile on his face.

"You had a bigger target," Pauling replied.

They quickly left the tunnel and headed for the Cadillac.

Pauling looked at Tallon.

"Veronica," she said.

Tallon said, "Yep."

CHAPTER TWENTY-EIGHT

Having defended some of the most nefarious mobsters in Chicago's past decades, Peter Kleinfeld knew a thing or two about their habits. Where they liked to eat. How they handled their extramarital affairs. And where they liked to hide out when the heat was on.

One go-to move was to hide in a boat whose paperwork did not list you as the owner.

Reason being, especially in the boating off-season – which for Chicago was nine months long – practically few people if any were using the harbor. Once the ice began to set, all boats would be out, but it was too early.

So inside *Best Defense*, a 65-foot yacht owned

by a shell company of his law firm with his name nowhere to be found, Kleinfeld stirred a gin and tonic for Mary Chang, and a scotch on the rocks for himself.

They'd been hiding out in the boat ever since the latest news had come in regarding Stone's whereabouts.

"I wish it were summer," Chang said. "We could just head up to Mackinaw Island or something. Get out of town. Just eat, drink and screw."

"That would be nice," Kleinfeld said. "A great place to hide out. Sleep on the boat, go into town for dinner. No wiseguys for hundreds of miles. No one around to hear you scream when I'm doing you from behind."

Chang sipped from her drink as her lover grinned at her, his face full of lascivious greed.

"How are we going to spin it when they finally kill him and someone starts asking about what happened at the prison?" Chang asked, spoiling the moment. Kleinfeld's face returned to its normal, pensive self.

"We have no idea what happened in that prison, of course," he said. He sat on the red, white and blue pinstriped bench across from Chang. "The men who attacked Stone are dead.

And we had nothing to do with the security guard's murder."

"But..."

"But nothing," Kleinfeld said. His eyes focused on Chang. She could be a little weak at times. Deep down, he felt she didn't show him enough appreciation for where she was today. Without him pulling strings, and setting up Vito Barranca for murder, she never would have gotten the gig as Chicago's top prosecutor. That was okay. He had big enough balls for both of them.

"Look, it was Junior who came to us with the plan to whack his father and use Stone Morticelli as the scapegoat," he reasoned. "The Feds needed someone to lock up once Senior was dead and they had no real meat left to their case. And Stone was too popular, and too good at what he did with the rest of the crew. He was competition and the old man liked Stone more than he liked Junior."

"No one likes Junior," Chang pointed out.

"True."

"I know I don't," Stone said.

Kleinfeld dropped his glass of scotch and Chang let out a shriek.

Kleinfeld's first thought was *how did he know about this boat?*

"Veronica told me," Stone said, as if Kleinfeld had asked the question out loud. "When we came up with the plan to make it look like I was going to meet with Lauren Pauling."

"And why would Veronica do that?" His eyes were shifting back and forth as his mind struggled to make sense of the situation.

"Because she's sleeping with Junior, of course," Stone said. "You didn't know that?"

Kleinfeld looked into Stone's cold blue eyes. He looked even bigger than he remembered. Prison had made him tougher, even more danger- ous. Kleinfeld hadn't thought that possible.

Well, he was a defense attorney, one of the best ever. If he couldn't talk his way out of–

Stone crossed the room and placed his hands on Kleinfeld's throat.

The defense attorney struggled to open his mouth. "Now Stone–" he choked out.

The crack filled the expensive boat's sump- tuous cabin as Stone broke Kleinfeld's neck in two.

Chang shrieked again.

Stone reached inside Kleinfeld's suit coat and took out a small .38 automatic. He turned to look at Chang.

"Will the defendant please rise?" he asked.

Chang got to her feet, her knees wobbled. Her hands shook.

Stone shot her twice in the chest.

CHAPTER TWENTY-NINE

The security guard manning the information desk at Veronica Morticelli's luxury high-rise recognized Pauling and waved her and Tallon through. The elevator doors opened and they stepped inside. Pauling punched the button for the penthouse.

On the way up, they each double-checked their weapons.

"Locked and loaded," Tallon said.

The elevator stopped and the doors opened. Pauling stepped into the marble lobby.

The two bodyguards outside Veronica's oversized French doors were no longer standing. They were face down, on top of matching pools of crimson red.

"Shit," Tallon said. He and Pauling both walked forward, approached the door.

"Come in, it's open!" a man's voice called out full of cheer.

Pauling went in first and spotted the man in the nicely tailored suit. Her pulse was steady but she was on edge. This all felt wrong. Like it was a trap.

"My name is Brooks," the man said. He glanced over at Veronica, seated next to him on the same white leather couch she'd been in when they last spoke. But this time, Pauling noticed her head was tilted back and a crude red line was drawn across her throat, with blood cascading down onto the front of a cashmere sweater.

"Please, don't get up, Veronica," Brooks said.

"Why did you kill her?" Pauling asked.

"He didn't," a voice said. "I did."

In the Bureau, Pauling had been trained for many different kinds of scenarios. One of them was how to deal with a situation involving multiple armed combatants. In this case, the voice was off to Pauling's right. Tallon was also on her right side.

As tempting as it was to glance in the direction of the new voice, she didn't. For various reasons. One, if the person represented a threat, Tallon was in a better position to address it.

Two. The man in front of her was armed. She knew that. He had been sitting turned slightly to the side, favoring his right arm. She knew in the nanosecond it took for her to hear the voice on her right, the man in the suit would wait for their focus to shift and then shoot them both.

Pauling didn't turn.

Instead, she raised her pistol at the same time as the man next to Veronica.

They both fired.

Pauling heard a grunt behind her as she fired more rounds at the man in the suit. Next to her, she heard Tallon's gun roaring.

The man in the suit fell to the floor and rolled.

Pauling knew she'd hit him–

Something struck her hard from behind and she crashed to the floor. A shadow leapt over her and as she rolled to her feet, she saw Stone Morticelli race across the room. He sprang forward and landed on top of the man on the ground. Stone had his hands out, and placed them on either side of the man's head.

Crack.

Even with her ears ringing from the gunshots,

the smell of burnt powder in the air, she heard the man's neck break in two.

Stone toppled off the dead man and Pauling swiveled to Tallon. He stood over the lifeless body of Vito Barranca Jr.

"Jesus," Tallon said. "Is Chicago always like this?"

Pauling approached the three bodies at the other end of the room. The man in the suit who'd fired a shot at her must have hit Stone in the chest. Because Morticelli was on his back, his entire front covered in blood.

Pauling looked at the logo: Milwaukee Bucks.

The man in the suit was dead. Pauling had no idea who he was but it was clear he'd been sent to take out Veronica.

Pauling stepped over to the woman. The man in the suit had certainly done his job. Very thorough.

She crossed the room back to where Tallon stood, looking down at Vito Jr.

Outside the room, they heard the elevator open and then footsteps raced toward them.

"FBI!" someone shouted.

FBI Agent Helm appeared in the doorway, his gun drawn, a team of agents behind him. He saw

Pauling and Tallon, lowered his weapon and signaled for his men to do the same.

"Good Christ," he said, surveying the carnage. "Looks like we're a little late."

Pauling holstered her gun.

"Oh, you're just in time," she said.

"For what?"

"To take credit."

CHAPTER THIRTY

It was nearly two days before the endless interviews with the Bureau wrapped up. Tallon and Pauling returned to New York and to her loft. She filled the huge French bathtub and Tallon brought in an ice-cold bottle of champagne. They both stripped off their clothes and sank into the hot soapy water. Pauling had lit a candle at each end and soft music played in the background.

"I've got a question or two," he said. He poured them each a glass of champagne. They sat opposite each other.

"After Stone shot Kleinfeld and Chang, he raced to Veronica's apartment. Was he going to kill her? Or say goodbye?"

"My guess is he was going to make up for the lost time he'd spent in prison, *then* kill her."

Tallon sipped his champagne. All thoughts of his ranch out west were gone. He could stay in this tub with Pauling forever.

"So Kleinfeld saw an opportunity within Junior's plan to get his lover into an even more powerful position that would benefit both himself and his clients."

"Yes. In hindsight, we couldn't have known that, but still..." Pauling said.

"And then after waiting just the right amount of time, they decided to tie up loose ends. Or, loose end, in this case. You'd gone back to New York. Stone was in prison. And the newspapers had stopped writing about the case. Old news. Forgotten."

Pauling nodded. "They weren't really worried about Stone talking. They were worried about him getting out. They'd pushed for maximum security while making it look like they were doing the opposite. But even Kleinfeld couldn't manage it because the charges weren't there. A perfectionist like Kleinfeld couldn't take the risk of Stone eventually getting out. So he hired the Corsicans to kill Stone and in the end, that was his downfall. Because Stone killed them, and then

Kleinfeld had to hire a killer named Brooks to try to finish the job, along with Veronica."

"And her boyfriend, Junior, decided to use Veronica to lure Stone in and have his thugs kill him."

"And Veronica tried to use us. She called me, but it was at Junior's urging."

Tallon smacked his lips and poured himself another glass.

"What's that saying about the best-laid plans..."

"They do tend to go awry," Pauling said.

She rubbed Tallon's thighs and leaned forward.

"Speaking of plans," she said.

Tallon had closed his eyes, luxuriating in the moment, but now they snapped back open.

"Yeah?"

"When are we going back to your ranch?" she asked.

He smiled at her.

She leaned closer and said, "You know, when are we going back...home?"

BUY THE NEXT BOOK IN THE SERIES! THE JACK REACHER CASES - BOOK 15!

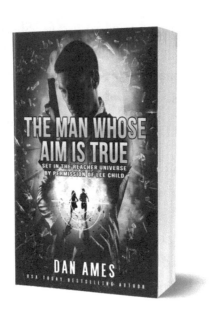

AuthorDanAmes.com

A USA TODAY BESTSELLING BOOK

Book One in The JACK REACHER Cases

AuthorDanAmes.com

A FAST-PACED ACTION-PACKED THRILLER SERIES

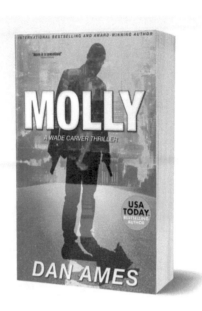

AuthorDanAmes.com

AN AWARD-WINNING BESTSELLING MYSTERY SERIES

Buy DEAD WOOD, the first John Rockne Mystery.

AuthorDanAmes.com

"Fast-paced, engaging, original."
-*NY Times bestselling author Thomas Perry*

ABOUT THE AUTHOR

Dan Ames is a USA TODAY Bestselling Author, Amazon Kindle #1 bestseller, GoodReads Readers Choice finalist and winner of the Independent Book Award for Crime Fiction.

www.authordanames.com
dan@authordanames.com

ALSO BY DAN AMES

THE JACK REACHER CASES

The JACK REACHER Cases #1 (A Hard Man To Forget)

The JACK REACHER Cases #2 (The Right Man For Revenge)

The JACK REACHER Cases #3 (A Man Made For Killing)

The JACK REACHER Cases #4 (The Last Man To Murder)

The JACK REACHER Cases #5 (The Man With No Mercy)

The JACK REACHER Cases #6 (A Man Out For Blood)

The JACK REACHER Cases #7 (A Man Beyond The Law)

The JACK REACHER Cases #8 (The Man Who Walks Away)

The JACK REACHER Cases (The Man Who Strikes Fear)

The JACK REACHER Cases (The Man Who Stands Tall)

The JACK REACHER Cases (The Man Who Works Alone)

The Jack Reacher Cases (A Man Built For Justice)

The JACK REACHER Cases #13 (A Man Born for Battle)

The JACK REACHER Cases #14 (The Perfect Man for Payback)

The JACK REACHER Cases #15 (The Man Whose Aim Is True)

The JACK REACHER Cases #16 (The Man Who Dies Here)

The JACK REACHER Cases #17 (The Man With Nothing To Lose)

The JACK REACHER Cases #18 (The Man Who Never Goes Back)

The JACK REACHER Cases #19 (The Man From The Shadows)

The JACK REACHER CASES #20 (The Man Behind The Gun)

JACK REACHER'S SPECIAL INVESTIGATORS

BOOK ONE: DEAD MEN WALKING

BOOK TWO: GAME OVER

BOOK THREE: LIGHTS OUT

BOOK FOUR: NEVER FORGIVE, NEVER FORGET

BOOK FIVE: HIT THEM FAST, HIT THEM HARD

BOOK SIX: FINISH THE FIGHT

THE JOHN ROCKNE MYSTERIES

DEAD WOOD (John Rockne Mystery #1)

HARD ROCK (John Rockne Mystery #2)

COLD JADE (John Rockne Mystery #3)

LONG SHOT (John Rockne Mystery #4)

EASY PREY (John Rockne Mystery #5)

BODY BLOW (John Rockne Mystery #6)

THE WADE CARVER THRILLERS

MOLLY (Wade Carver Thriller #1)

SUGAR (Wade Carver Thriller #2)

ANGEL (Wade Carver Thriller #3)

THE WALLACE MACK THRILLERS

THE KILLING LEAGUE (Wallace Mack Thriller #1)

THE MURDER STORE (Wallace Mack Thriller #2)

FINDERS KILLERS (Wallace Mack Thriller #3)

THE MARY COOPER MYSTERIES

DEATH BY SARCASM (Mary Cooper Mystery #1)

MURDER WITH SARCASTIC INTENT (Mary Cooper Mystery #2)

GROSS SARCASTIC HOMICIDE (Mary Cooper Mystery #3)

THE CIRCUIT RIDER (WESTERNS)

THE CIRCUIT RIDER (Circuit Rider #1)

KILLER'S DRAW (Circuit Rider #2)

THE RAY MITCHELL THRILLERS

THE RECRUITER

KILLING THE RAT

HEAD SHOT

STANDALONE THRILLERS:

KILLER GROOVE (Rockne & Cooper Mystery #1)

BEER MONEY (Burr Ashland Mystery #1)

TO FIND A MOUNTAIN (A WWII Thriller)

BOX SETS:

AMES TO KILL

GROSSE POINTE PULP

GROSSE POINTE PULP 2

TOTAL SARCASM

WALLACE MACK THRILLER COLLECTION

.

SHORT STORIES:

THE GARBAGE COLLECTOR

BULLET RIVER

SCHOOL GIRL

HANGING CURVE

SCALE OF JUSTICE

FREE BOOKS AND MORE

**Would you like a FREE copy
of my story BULLET RIVER and the
chance
to win a free Kindle?**

**Then sign up for the DAN AMES BOOK
CLUB:**

AuthorDanAmes.com

THE MAN WHOSE AIM IS TRUE

SET IN THE REACHER UNIVERSE
BY PERMISSION OF LEE CHILD

DAN AMES

USA TODAY BESTSELLING AUTHOR

PRAISE FOR DAN AMES

"Fast-paced, engaging, original."

— NEW YORK TIMES
BESTSELLING AUTHOR
THOMAS PERRY

"Ames is a sensation among readers who love fast-paced thrillers."

— MYSTERY TRIBUNE

"Cuts like a knife."

— SAVANNAH MORNING NEWS

"Furiously paced. Great action."

— NEW YORK TIMES
BESTSELLING AUTHOR BEN
LIEBERMAN

A USA TODAY BESTSELLING BOOK

Book One in The JACK REACHER Cases

AUTHORDANAMES.COM

FREE BOOKS AND MORE

**Would you like a FREE copy
of my story BULLET RIVER and the
chance
to win a free Kindle?**

**Then sign up for the DAN AMES BOOK
CLUB:**

AUTHORDANAMES.COM

THE MAN WHOSE AIM IS TRUE

The Jack Reacher Cases #15

by

Dan Ames

But from each crime are born bullets
that one
day seek out in you where the heart lies.
-*Pablo Neruda*

CHAPTER ONE

Moments before his head was blown apart by a sniper's perfectly placed bullet, the older man opened the gate to the dog park.

He was probably in his early sixties, wearing dark brown corduroy pants, a heavy sweater and a black jacket, unzipped. Although his shoulders were stooped, he had a keen, clear gaze and moved with a quiet confidence.

The dog park was a tiny square of green bordered on all sides by rows of neat and highly desirable Brooklyn brownstones. At one end was a set of picnic tables and a second, fenced-in area for larger dogs. At several locations were cylindrical waste baskets and plastic bags designed to deal with by-products from man's best friend.

The sky was baby blue tinged with mile-high borders of cirrus streaks, and a faint breeze blew the few remaining strands of white hair lazily above the old man's ears. It was cool, but not cold and the sounds of several dogs barking punctuated the otherwise serene-like setting.

The Schipperke Terrier on the end of the old man's leash was happy to see his old friend, an Italian Greyhound named Sal who was about his same size. He strained against his leash, eager to get inside the fence and start the best part of his day.

When the bullet hit – a custom round larger and more powerful than its nearest relative, the .300 Winchester Magnum, traveling at nearly 2,800 feet per second – the little dog both felt and heard the impact. The Schipperke's name was Churchy, named after the old man's idol Winston Churchill. Churchy had never heard that particular sound before and suddenly the firmness on the other end of the leash was gone.

The smell of blood reached the dog's nose and something primal triggered his fear. He darted back to his owner who was now on the ground. Churchy barked, but it was as if no one could hear him.

He kept barking but the man he viewed as the

leader of their pack, remained still. The smell was something unique to Churchy.

A high-pitched scream startled the dog, and soon, there were more screams and shouts and then a high-pitched wailing followed by flashing red lights.

Churchy had a feeling he wouldn't be playing with his friend today, after all.

CHAPTER TWO

War criminal.

Lauren Pauling stared at the words on her computer screen. She sat in her home office, in her loft on Barrow Street in New York City. Her hair was pulled back and she hadn't changed out of her workout clothes: yoga pants and a sports bra.

Pauling had been going through her email, which to her surprise, hadn't slowed down even after the sale of her security firm. As often as she unsubscribed from junk email, it seemed there were new ones ready to replace them.

Once she discarded all of the trash messages, she finally opened the one email she actually wanted to read. It was from an old friend at her former place of employment: the Federal Bureau of Investigation.

Pauling hadn't been with the FBI for years now; in fact, she'd started, built and sold her firm in the intervening time period. But she still kept in touch with some of her colleagues. A few, actually, as in very few.

But Deborah Haskins had been one of her best friends. Pauling had been her senior and she'd mentored Haskins and the two had grown very close. Haskins was probably nearing the end of her career with the Bureau, something Pauling knew her friend was viewing with mixed feelings.

Pauling read the email and sat back in her chair, stunned.

She read it a second time.

There were two words and a name that had shocked her.

The words were *war criminal*.

They certainly weren't new to Pauling. She'd targeted, arrested and helped put away more than a few war criminals in her lifetime.

No, those two words weren't what had given her a shock, enough to drain the blood from her face.

It was the name that followed.

Jack Reacher.

CHAPTER THREE

Within moments of verifying through his rifle scope that the old man's head had indeed been blown into many different directions, the sniper calmly disassembled his one-of-a-kind rifle and placed it in a very generic-looking backpack.

This was not the sort of throwaway weapon one left at the scene to avoid being tied to the crime by authorities.

Not considering how much time, money and effort had been put into designing and customizing the rifle.

The cool, detached demeanor required to make the shot was beginning to dissolve in the shooter's mind. This kill hadn't been an anonymous Taliban fighter in the mountains of Afghanistan.

This kill had meant something.

Emotion, which was something snipers were trained to keep locked down under all circumstances, was beginning to show.

He walked calmly from the rooftop to the access door, then descended the stairs that led to the rear of the building.

As he pushed open the metal door he heard the first of the sirens. This was New York, after all. A man's head getting blown off in a crowded dog park would not go unnoticed for long. The man walked calmly down the alley and turned to his right along the street, away from the kill site.

He had on a black baseball cap, blue jeans, black steel-toed boots and a three-quarters length olive green jacket. He'd slipped on a pair of mirrored aviator sunglasses. His beard was neatly trimmed. He was tall, but not strikingly so, and solidly built, but not overly muscular. To the untrained eye, he simply looked like a well-built, athletic man dressed in a fairly nondescript way.

The rental car was parked on a side street devoid of any bank or store cameras pointed at the street. He'd made sure to put enough time on the meter to avoid being flagged by a traffic cop for a parking ticket and leaving any trace of his presence.

The shooter unlocked the driver's side door and placed the backpack in the passenger seat. He could've put it in the trunk, but he preferred to keep it close to him. Old habits died hard and if need be, he wanted to be able to grab his pack and go, not fumble with the trunk fob.

The sniper was known as Rider, although that was a nickname bestowed upon him in his youth, due to a local legend about a ghost that haunted a legendary, remote road far from the small town in which he grew up. The ghost was rumored to be able to change shape and appearance at will, and was blamed for several strange deaths that had occurred in the town over the years.

No one knew the origin of the name, but the prevailing rumor was that it was the name of a young man who'd been murdered in the 1800s and now haunted the area.

Rider had chosen the name as his sniper handle in the military, although most didn't know its origin.

That was fine with him.

Anonymity was key.

As he drove the rental car away from the

scene, he felt a surge of satisfaction, and a blood thirst.

It was a thirst that would soon be quenched again.

Because Rider was just getting started.

CHAPTER FOUR

After an exchange of emails with her former colleague at the Bureau, Pauling arranged a meeting over a cup of coffee to discuss the ridiculous story that Jack Reacher may have committed a war crime.

The place was called Perk Avenue and was only a few blocks from Pauling's loft. It was a neighborhood joint with a few tables on the sidewalk, and a half-dozen inside. Pauling chose the table at the back of the restaurant out of habit. She rarely felt comfortable dining outside, unless it was a courtyard-type setting or perhaps a café in a small town. There was something about the combination of being somewhat compromised when dining and also sitting so close to the busy streets of New York that didn't mesh well with Pauling.

When she was discussing matters that could possibly land herself or a current employee of the FBI into murky waters, she definitely chose the most private option available.

Special Agent Deborah Haskins entered the coffee shop, ordered an espresso and joined Pauling at the table.

"Pauling," Haskins said.

"Hey," Pauling said. Her friend was a tall, willowy brunette with a lean face and a sharp nose. There were touches of gray in her hair and Pauling couldn't help but think about the deadly combination of sexism and ageism that sometimes occurred at the Bureau. It was much better now, but early in Pauling's career, it had been rampant.

Haskins had survived this long and Pauling knew the woman was bright, assertive and ambitious. She was also principled which sometimes caused issues in the short term but Pauling was optimistic enough to believe in the long run, it was the only way to go.

"You look good. Retirement suits you," Haskins said. Pauling had kept her friend up to

date with her post-Bureau life; the firm she'd sold
and now, a sort of limbo that technically was
retirement. In Pauling's mind, she would never
actually retire. She was simply waiting for something to steer her to her next passion.

Her mind naturally went to Michael Tallon,
her current significant other, who was presently
at his small ranch near Death Valley.

"Thanks, idle hands, as they say," Pauling
smiled.

They each sipped the drink – Pauling had
opted for a latte.

"How are things at the office?" Pauling asked.
She wasn't particularly interested in the usual
shenanigans and politics associated with life in
the FBI, but she didn't want to dive right into the
real reason for the meeting just yet.

Haskins filled her in on her current case: a
shady hedge fund manager who was most likely
laundering money for a Russian oligarch.

"How about you?" Haskins asked after she'd
given Pauling all of the sordid details of the case,
including a private jet filled with underage
Russian girls.

"I've had a few interesting things come up but
lately it's been quiet. The calm before the storm,
maybe, based on your message."

Pauling was referring to Haskins' message that someone had claimed Jack Reacher was a war criminal.

"Very strange, that one," Haskins said. "So here's what happened: I'd flagged a whole bunch of stuff related to the Russian oligarch I'm investigating. He had ties to Afghanistan, including some reputed bounties placed on both US and UK soldiers."

Haskins sipped her espresso and leveled her gaze at Pauling.

"One of my alerts tripped a communiqué in Russian that seemed to imply an American soldier was guilty, or at least accused of, war crimes," Haskins explained. "He was in the Army. An MP. And his name was Jack Reacher."

Pauling shook her head. "Impossible, but tell me what else you learned."

"Honestly, not much," Haskins said. "It seems that someone at some point was investigating war crimes committed by Army soldiers, most likely in Afghanistan, although that wasn't totally clear. What those actual crimes were, if they were even actually committed, wasn't included. Nothing else really was."

"It seems much more likely to me that Reacher was the one *investigating* the crimes.

After all, that's what he did in the Army," Pauling pointed out. "He was for all intents and purposes a homicide investigator. And besides, I know him and there was no way he would be involved in that kind of thing as a participant. An investigator sure, but a participant, no."

Haskins pulled a slip of paper from her purse. "I transposed this by hand because I didn't want to send it to the printer."

Pauling knew what she meant: printing something at the FBI meant it was permanently in the record. If the document ever became an issue, it could be traced straight back to the computer that had sent it to the printer.

"Obviously, I know about your history with Reacher so that's why I contacted you," Haskins said. "I also did a quick check of Reacher's record – there's no sign of any active investigation. In fact, his file has been totally inactive for years now."

Pauling nodded. She had told Haskins about Reacher, an indication of how close they'd been. The bond was still there, thankfully.

Pauling slid the note into her pocket.

"Thank you, Deb," Pauling said. "I appreciate it."

Haskins smiled and polished off her espresso. She got to her feet. "No problem. I figure if anyone can get to the bottom of it, you can."

Pauling smiled back.

"That's exactly what I'm going to do."

CHAPTER FIVE

NYPD homicide detective Claire Brewster studied the crime scene and shook her head. She was one of the most consistent cops on the homicide squad when it came to keeping up on the range. She knew her weapons, her ballistics and the many calculations required to estimate the type of kill she was looking at.

As she studied the crime scene at the dog park, where an older man had clearly been shot in the head by a very powerful weapon, she considered the evidence.

It was the power of the weapon that surprised her. A ten-year veteran of the homicide squad, Claire was no stranger to violent crime. She'd been a cop all her life, raised by two

Irish parents who believed in law and order. Her ex-husband could testify to Claire's passion for the job. It was her absence around the house that, according to him, had triggered his departure. Although Claire figured it was the new secretary at his firm that had been the icing on the cake.

"What the hell was this guy using, an elephant gun?" she asked the crime scene tech, a slim Asian man named Kev. She didn't know if that was short for something, or a nickname or maybe she was mispronouncing it, but she didn't care enough to ask. Plus, these days everyone was offended by anything related to one's nationality, so Claire left it alone.

"All I can tell you is that it wasn't a .50 cal. I've seen a couple of those and there would be nothing left," Kev said. His voice was high and raspy, like a female lounge singer from the Fifties.

"It couldn't have been that much smaller," Claire said. "This is more damage than I think I've ever seen."

"Not even close for me," Kev said. "One time, a guy went to Home Depot and brought back a wood chipper to get rid of his roommate. They lived together in a studio apartment. Talk about avant-garde decorating."

The crime scene tech giggled and Claire ignored him.

"How soon will we have ballistics?"

"Considering the situation, I expect this case will be pushed to the top."

Claire knew what he meant; an old man shot down in a dog park, probably by a man with a rifle, was certain to make news. Public scrutiny brought a certain motivation to the political machinery of the NYPD.

Kev finished processing the scene and soon the body was hauled away. Claire worked the witnesses again, and did some door to door. A woman with a Standard Poodle said she'd been walking toward the old man because he was notorious for not picking up his dog's poop. She had intended to confront the issue when the man's head had literally disintegrated in a shower of blood, flesh and bone. Obviously, the woman explained, she felt no need to be concerned after that.

On the bright side, Claire had been able to learn the identity of the victim: one Victor Panko, who lived less than three blocks from the park.

Claire drove her unmarked car to the old man's Brooklyn brownstone. *Nice digs*, she thought.

The front door was locked and no one answered the doorbell. No neighbors came out to check. Claire rang the bell on each neighbor's house but no one answered those, either.

She walked around to the back. There was no garage but instead, a parking space directly behind the building. Parked there was an old Lincoln sedan. Silver. At least fifteen years old but clean. Claire guessed it had low miles and that the engine still packed a punch. She was sure it belonged to Panko – the Lincoln was an old man's car if she'd ever seen one.

She jotted down the license plate and sent it in for confirmation.

Claire wished there was a way she could get inside, but she would have to wait. Until then, she would have to find out all she could about Victor Panko and why someone would want to blow off his head with a high-powered rifle.

She put her car into gear and headed back toward the office.

CHAPTER SIX

The feeling was familiar: frustration.

Ever since Lauren Pauling had met and fallen hard for Jack Reacher, she'd felt a vague sense of frustration. It wasn't that she was still in love with him – in fact, their time together had been so brief that she wasn't even sure she'd had *time* to fall in love with him.

No, Pauling was confident she'd never actually completed that arc; Reacher had stormed into her life and then simply walked out of it. Even back then, she was a mature woman, smart enough and experienced enough to know that he wasn't the kind of man to settle down behind a white picket fence.

Still, no one had ever so completely disappeared from her life like Jack Reacher. He had no fixed address. No car. No cell phone. Certainly no computer and, therefore, wasn't on any type of social media. Hell, Reacher probably hadn't even heard of Facebook or Twitter.

The only real way to trace Reacher was to maybe track down his ATM withdrawals, but that required supreme effort in getting into a bank's records and Pauling had no desire to do that, just yet. It would have to be a dire emergency to take that step.

Pauling wasn't about to panic on Reacher's behalf just because his name had been mentioned in connection with a war crime. In fact, the cool head she still possessed from her time with the Bureau pointed out she had no information there was even an active investigation into possible crimes against her favorite wanderer. Just an intercepted message, chatter over a wire, about something that possibly occurred, but also just as plausibly hadn't taken place.

Having said that, Pauling wasn't the type of woman to ignore it. She still felt connected enough to Reacher and if someone she cared about was possibly being linked to heinous crimes, Pauling wasn't about to wash her hands of the information.

Besides, as Haskins had pointed out, she was retired.

Tallon was at his ranch, and she had spent the last month focused on exercising, eating right and spending time at the range. She loved to shoot and had been experimenting with a new gun: a Colt single action army revolver nicknamed the "Peacemaker."

Deep in her heart, however, she knew she needed something more serious to tackle, and this strange development with Reacher, as unfortunate as it was, fit the bill.

Pauling went back to her loft and headed straight for her home office. It was a small space tucked at one end of the apartment and was outfitted for privacy. She'd had a desk custom made and a wall unit that housed her library as well as several locked compartments for her weapons.

Now, Pauling pulled herself up to her desktop computer and fired it up. Like any organized investigator, she already had a file on Reacher. It had basically been a place to collect the documents from when they had worked together, briefly, years ago. Since then, she'd occasionally received word of some of his escapades and downloaded any notation of them and copied them into the folder.

What she was interested in now, though, was his service record. That, too, was on her desktop in a folder creatively labeled "Reacher."

She opened the documents and reread them, although there was nothing new. She'd spent probably way too much time reading them after he'd gone. He'd been an exemplary investigator, which she already knew, and had climbed the ranks until he'd had a minor setback and then, a few years later, he'd been 'made redundant' as they say.

What interested Pauling was any sign that Reacher had been in Afghanistan.

She scoured all of the paperwork in his file and came to a very clear answer: he had not.

Inwardly, she sighed a small amount of relief. Pauling knew there was no way in hell Reacher was a war criminal, the man was an overgrown boy scout, always doing the right thing and helping out those in need. Reacher hated bullies, had an intense dislike of them so much that he often punched them into the next universe.

Still, it bothered Pauling that someone had made the suggestion.

And why had they?

Pauling knew what she had to do next: study Reacher's cases, or those of his unit. Maybe they had been involved in Afghanistan, without Reacher's involvement.

For that, she would have to go beyond her own desktop folder.

She would have to access records in the Pentagon.

Thankfully, she knew just the person to help her.

CHAPTER SEVEN

Detective Claire Brewster stood on the rooftop and watched the dog park in the distance. According to Kev, based on caliber of the bullet, trajectory at impact, and blood splatter, the shooter had been most likely on this rooftop.

It was a building like any other in New York: the ground floor held some retail shops and the rest were overpriced apartments. The rooftop held nothing but a few exhaust vents, gravel, and pigeon crap.

The problem for Claire was that nothing else had been found on the rooftop by the crime scene techs. They'd already dusted and photographed and measured, but to no avail. They'd found literally nothing, save for one possible foot scrape near the spot where the shooter may have set up his rifle. It was the slightest scuff, black, probably from a boot. They had photographed it, but there wasn't much else they could do. A million kinds of shoes, sneakers or boots could make a mark like that. And the fact that it was only an inch or so from the ground level meant nothing in terms of giving any indication into the shooter's size.

Claire tamped down her frustration and grabbed her iPad. She scrolled through the ballistics report that had just arrived.

It made for interesting reading. The caliber of bullet was still undetermined, but the ballistics expert, a man named Dawson, had put forth a theory that it was a Russian round, rarely used, and somewhat experimental. It was loosely known by an acronym RKN74. The report didn't explain what the hell that acronym stood for but Claire made a mental note to find out.

In some ways, that was good news. The more unusual the weapon or ammo, the easier it would be to trace. "Easier" being a relative term. Simply put, it was better than the bullet being a .223, a .30-06 or a .308 Winchester. The most common sniper rifle in the world, Claire knew, was a 700 Remington (renamed the M24 by the military).

Still, the rifle was unknown. Claire would have

to talk to the weapons expert and find out what kind of rifle could fire this RKN74.

In the meantime, she had work to do. If the shooter had chosen this spot, then it meant that he'd scouted Victor Panko's habits and knew the old man took his dog to the park every day. Which meant the shooter must have spent some time here. She went back down to the lobby and studied the directory.

It was an apartment building with some retail shops on the first floor. There was a guitar repair shop, nail salon and a real estate office. She talked to the owners of all three and got nowhere.

Next, she went into the lobby and sat. As residents walked in with bags of groceries or shopping bags, or even better, dogs, Claire asked them if they'd seen a man in the past few days or weeks who seemed out of place. Especially one with any kind of bag, or a long, rectangular case.

No one knew anything.

Until the old lady appeared out of nowhere. She had on a pink fur coat and carried a white poodle.

"Yes, indeed I saw a young man here two days in a row," the old lady said.

Claire got out her notebook.

"I said hello to him and he nodded back," the

old lady continued. "Didn't say a word, and he didn't look at Silly here."

"Silly?"

"My dog's name is Sylvia but I call her Silly."

The little poodle's head popped up at the sound of her name.

"What caught your attention?" Claire asked.

"He was a very fit young man, with sunglasses that had mirrors. He also had a neatly trimmed beard. That's important to me. I don't like the beards these men have where it's all unshaven and halfway down their neck. A neatly trimmed beard is a sign of class and very distinguished."

"I see."

"He had a backpack with him and I wondered if he was homeless, but then I figured not because of the nice beard. Oh, and he had a weird tattoo."

Clair raised an eyebrow.

"Tattoo?"

"Yes, when he reached his backpack after I tried to talk to him, his arm caught my eye and there was a big scary thing on his arm. It was a horrible thing. It looked like a skull with flames and a gun. The whole thing scared me and I think Silly was scared, too. She growled which she never does and then she whimpered. I realized he was no nice young man. Probably a bad person. That's what made me remember him when you asked."

Claire thanked the old lady and Silly, got her information and spent two more hours asking questions but no one provided anything new. She headed back toward the station.

All she had was a tattoo.

But it was better than nothing.

CHAPTER EIGHT

The custom seaplane floating in the turquoise blue waters just off the Bahamian mainland sported the name *Peregrine*. It was a vintage Boeing aircraft made for the Navy in the 1930s and had since been completely overhauled.

Instead of a utilitarian vessel devoid of personality, it had now been turned into a luxury hotel suite that could go airborne. It featured three spacious cabins, two bathrooms, an office and a complete host of electronics, including satellite communications enabling high-speed internet and cellular networks.

The plane's owner was also the pilot; a former pilot and member of the Special Forces.

He was a rugged man, broad in both shoulders

and chest, with a narrow waist and powerful legs. His hair was close-cropped and the color of gunmetal. His nose was flattened, and his teeth were straight and even, but dull in color as if tempered by years of whiskey and cigarettes.

The man, known by his online friends as Follett, was reading the crime report of an old man who'd been gunned down in New York City. Shot from long distance by a sniper, was the current hypothesis.

Follett sank into one of the leather club chairs that gave him a vantage point view of the water outside. The plane had a row of windows, the one through which he now looked was the biggest of them. It was his favorite spot in the aircraft, other than the bedroom.

The water was gorgeous, like topaz and as smooth as glass. In the distance, not even a wave rippled.

Usually, the sight of the water made him relaxed and peaceful, but the news was unsettling. He knew the man who'd been murdered. Knew him quite well, and the role he played in a certain organization.

Follett no longer felt calm.

He was triggered by the news article and he needed to take action. Anger was a form of arousal and he remembered with relish what he had in the bedroom.

For now, he pushed that idea aside.

This was bad news, there was no way around it; no way to spin it as some kind of opportunity, which is what Follett normally tried to do in dire circumstances. It's what he'd been trained to do.

Visually, he kept seeing the man he knew being shot in the head. Follett had seen long-distance head shots made by snipers under his command. He'd seen a great deal of them. He knew what hey looked like, what they even sounded like. How the victim's body crumpled after impact, half of the head blown to smithereens.

The dead man hadn't really been his friend, per se, more of a business associate.

They were partners, in a sense.

Follett heaved himself to his feet and walked into the bedroom.

On the bed was a very young man. His wrists and ankles were bound.

The youth looked up at him with fear.

Follett stripped off his shirt and dropped his swim trunks to reveal his highly excited manhood.

"I'll make them pay, eventually," he said. "But you'll do for now."

With nothing but empty ocean for miles around the seaplane, no one could hear the young man scream.

CHAPTER NINE

Congressman Hector Ortiz had provided his constituency with a major surprise long before the second occurred.

Nearly ten years earlier, he'd run as a huge underdog going against an established opponent who'd spent nearly twenty years in office. No one had given Ortiz a shot. His ideas were too controversial, his experience too profound, his skin color too dark.

But he'd pulled it off and become one of the youngest congressmen to ever take office.

That had been a long time ago and now, he pulled off a second surprise. He had just triumphantly submitted a bill to the house floor that would set new goals for clean energy, protection of the environment and voters' rights. It was, he positioned, a revolutionary moment. Everything would change, he told the young people. They cheered.

But Ortiz thought they were ignorant.

The bill didn't stand much chance of passing, but that wasn't the point; things were never as they seemed in Washington. Simply getting a bill to the floor, beginning dialogue and, more importantly, for Ortiz to say he'd gotten the legislation thus far was a victory in and of itself.

A political victory, even if nothing much good would come of it. Of course, in Ortiz's eyes, getting himself reelected for yet another term was a very good thing, indeed.

A lifelong bachelor, Congressman Ortiz had his assistant book him a table for four at his favorite eatery: a gourmet DC restaurant called *Selva* that was his standby favorite after any kind of success.

His guests would all be friends, none of whom would accompany him back to his penthouse bachelor pad not far from the Capitol.

Ortiz sat in the back of the black SUV with tinted, bulletproof windows.

He sipped from a glass of scotch as the big vehicle maneuvered its way to the restaurant. Tonight would be a very good night, a celebration of his latest and greatest accomplishment.

He would enjoy more scotch, a glass of wine, a great meal, lively conversation, and cap it off with a night of playtime back in his big bed.

The congressman was almost tempted to access some of his favorite images on his cell phone, but decided against it. One, he tried not to look at them at all. And second, even though it was his personal phone, not the one supplied by the taxpayer dollars, it was meant to be done carefully and selectively.

Besides, they were almost to *Selva*.

Ortiz drained the rest of his drink and waited for his driver to open the door. He could see through the darkened window that the doorman was already opening the restaurant door and he could imagine his favorite table; in the back, with a great view of anyone who came into the place. Waited on by not one, but two waiters who made sure to never leave anyone at Ortiz's table wanting.

The congressman stepped onto the pavement and heard the door to the SUV bang shut behind him.

The second bang was one Ortiz never heard.

Because before the sound arrived, the bullet that blew apart the congressman's head reached its target.

CHAPTER TEN

illing gets easier.

Someone told him that when he was first starting out and he'd hoped, at the time, that it wasn't true. He didn't want to be one of those guys who could bestow death upon another human being with utter detachment. Where killing someone was as mundane as taking out the garbage or flushing the toilet.

But the advice turned out to be absolutely correct.

And it became a truism much sooner than he would have liked.

It was almost as if the first man he'd killed, an enemy combatant, was the first and only time he'd contemplated what he'd done. After that, they had all just been more deaths. He still remembered that first kill. The rest of them?

Not at all.

He knew that he'd ended their lives with the pull of a trigger. All at long distance. From the end of his rifle.

But it was different now.

In a sense, the old man at the dog park and now the congressman were enemy combatants. Unarmed, of course. But they'd been waging their own kind of war for many years and now, both karma and a bullet had finally arrived. It had been fired a long time ago and had taken its time reaching the target, but that it did.

This one had definitely been trickier, what with the secret service in tow. So he'd taken some extra precautions. Backed out even further than usual which gave him plenty of time to pack up his weapon, descend to his rental car and disappear from the area before anyone even knew where to look.

For now, Rider was pleased with his progress.

He glanced over at the passenger seat, looked at the pack with his rifle.

Just the two of us once again, he thought.

His burner cell phone rang and he glanced at the screen, and remembered that he was wrong.

CHAPTER ELEVEN

Michael Tallon was careful not to skyline himself. Meaning, rather than run over the crest of a hill, he tried to run alongside it and wait for an opening that didn't bring him out on top of the rise and make him visible for miles on end.

It was an old habit and probably not necessary in his backyard – which was the ever empty expanse of Death Valley.

Still, today was different.

Because he was being followed.

There were no if, ands or buts about it; there was a superstition among men like Tallon that the feeling of being watched was real. Mountain men used to claim they had the ability, yet Tallon believed it to be true only because he believed in subconscious clues.

The image of something in one's peripheral vision that didn't necessarily register. A sound or a shadow felt, but not noticed on a conscious level.

These things could add up.

He was on the last mile of his run, heading back toward his ranch, when the feeling came to him. He'd stopped twice and pretended to adjust his shoe or catch his breath, peering behind him for any glimpse of something out of place. A shadow where it shouldn't belong, a shape that seemed wrong.

But there was nothing but desert rock and cactus and dust.

Now, he sprinted down a short incline and took one last look back over his shoulder, but this time while he was on the move.

The tactic worked.

Tallon finally saw his pursuer.

It was a mountain lion, less than a hundred yards away.

Tallon knew they didn't hunt humans as a normal course of business; they only targeted people when they were usually sick or starving or both. This one looked thin and Tallon considered letting the cat get close and then shooting him.

Instead, he jogged back to his ranch, all the time with his hand on the pistol at the back of his running shorts.

The cat was either too weak or lacked the desperation to actually attack.

Tallon reached the back of his ranch house – a modest adobe structure – and let himself in.

He retrieved his binoculars and studied the cat who had stopped, probably getting the scents of various human activities and dealing with alarm bells. Tallon could get a rifle and drop the cat now.

Instead, he watched and soon the mountain lion disappeared back into the foothills that were now burning red with the setting sun.

Tallon put his binoculars back, stripped off his sweat-drenched clothes and showered. Just as he was getting dressed, his cell phone buzzed with a text.

He glanced at the screen.

It was from one of his former special ops buddies and the message was simple:

Remember that dude who shot RKN74?

Tallon did, in fact, remember the man. Or, at least, he remembered the stories about him.

A second text popped up.

Think this was him?

Before Tallon could answer either message, a web link popped up.

It was to a news article.

Tallon read the headline: ***Elderly Brooklyn Man Shot by Sniper.***

CHAPTER TWELVE

D issecting a man's history was no easy task. Detective Claire Brewster didn't assume it would be, yet she was surprised at the degree of difficulty in getting past Victor Panko's most recent activities.

She read through what she had so far: Victor Panko was sixty-eight years old, single, with no children. He ran a charity that raised funds for an international humanitarian organization.

Claire studied the documents before her and knew it wouldn't suffice.

He had a history and it seemed New York had been his home for all of his life. But the information was surprisingly sparse.

She forwarded a request for more information on the charity itself, including names, addresses and company filings with a specialist at the NYPD who tracked down financial information. In the meantime, Claire would also do some snooping around.

Just as she was set to take the search warrant she had for Panko's apartment, an email popped up on her computer with a red flag attached.

She clicked on it and read about the assassination of a congressman in D.C.

Claire frowned – none of her cases had any political involvement.

She scrolled through the email, looking for the text that would be highlighted to indicate why she was flagged.

And then, near the end of the information, she saw the words:

RKN74.

CHAPTER THIRTEEN

J ack Reacher's unit had been the Army's
110th MP. All paperwork, case histories,
files and personnel records would be
stored digitally within the firewalls of the
Pentagon.

Pauling herself had no way to access them.
She'd maintained access to some of the FBI's
system thanks to a few loopholes exploited by a
former client of hers whose specialty was
breaching firewalls. It helped that Pauling had
been an employee of the FBI and it had been
more of a matter of keeping access, as opposed to
obtaining it illegally.

The Pentagon, however, was a whole different
ball game.

For that, she used a former client who'd been

wrongfully terminated by his employer. That
employer, a large multinational bank, had
employed him as a hacker. However, when he'd
uncovered a few shenanigans being employed by
the bank's upper management team, he'd been
fired, and framed for embezzling.

Pauling not only helped clear his name but she
also earned him tens of millions of dollars in an
out-of-court settlement.

Now he worked as a private consultant, and
did any jobs for which Pauling sought his
assistance. She reached out to him and asked him
to dig around for anything in Jack Reacher's official Army files, or his unit's files, that tied to
activity in Afghanistan. Activity that might
somehow be construed as criminal.

That done, she began to investigate what she
could: war crimes committed by the Army in
Afghanistan. Her decision to focus solely on the
Army was a bit of a risk; she knew that. The fact
of the matter was more and more teams in the
military, especially special ops, were a mixture of
different branches. Delta brushed shoulders with
SEAL teams. Green Berets might have a Navy
comms officer in their team.

Hell, there were even international teams
where Americans might have a Canadian or

Australian as part of the group. The British Special Air Service were legendary, and sometimes might rub shoulders with Americans.

So technically, a war crime could be committed by every branch of the military, even if their mission wasn't solely their responsibility.

But there was no way she could investigate them all. Not that there were hundreds of war crimes, but things were often handled internally and to snoop through the Army, Air Force, Marines, Navy and National Guard files would have been too much. It would be thousands and thousands of incidents, files and reports that would take a dozen investigators working around the clock.

She had no choice but to focus only on one branch.

Besides, Jack Reacher had been Army and to her knowledge, MPs weren't often included as part of a multi-branch team. They tended to work alone.

What gave her some hope was that for an incident to be elevated to the status of war crime, it had to be something out of the ordinary. Not a case of friendly fire, or a questionable military action.

Additionally, as Reacher was being flagged as a

war criminal, the first organization to look at would be the Army. If nothing came of it, maybe she would widen her net, but she didn't think that was going to be the case.

Pauling began with public databases, including news organizations and LexisNexis, using search terms *war crimes, Afghanistan, criminal, murder*, etc.

What came back was fairly minimal, a fact that surprised Pauling.

There had been a massacre of an Afghani family by a psychopath and his team. The retaliation had been just as bad: an entire squad had been wiped out by local Afghanis. The investigation had been above board and conclusive, thoroughly covered with all perpetrators known and accounted for.

There was no mention of Reacher.

Sexual assaults had been plentiful; but again, nothing major and no sign of a wider conspiracy.

No, to be labeled a war crime, Pauling reasoned, it would have to be something especially heinous.

And that meant it would almost certainly be newsworthy – if the information was ever made public.

And so far, she'd found nothing.

Pauling closed down her computer and paced her loft apartment.

She decided to retrieve her new pal: the Colt Peacemaker, and head to the range. Shooting at targets helped her think.

Maybe as she was blowing away imaginary bad guys, she might think of a way to catch a real one.

CHAPTER FOURTEEN

Follett dumped the body of the young man at sea. He felt nothing as he watched the adolescent sink down to the bottom of the Atlantic, wrapped in chains.

From his vantage point on the deck of the seaplane *Peregrine*, Follett knew no one would find anything as he wasn't far from the Gulf Stream, the warm current of water that accounted for so much life in the ocean. The scent of the youth's blood and rotting flesh would draw carnivores from all depths of the waters and within days if not hours, nothing would be left.

Follett secured all of the doors and windows on the plane, making sure there was no trace of the youth's existence on board. He would do a second, even more thorough sterilization of the interior when he landed back in the US. Or, more accurately, his staff would see to it.

The big engines of the plane came to life and soon he was lifting off from the water. He'd spent a small fortune refurbishing the plane. It had come into this world decades ago mostly as first a military transport plane and then a few years later as a commercial cargo hauler before it was listed for sale.

It sat for years garnering little interest and Follett was able to acquire it for far below the asking price. He spent millions upgrading all aspects of the plane, both mechanical and aesthetic, to make it worthy of a private jet. But he liked the anonymity of the ocean, being able to land anywhere he wanted.

Now, he headed for his private hangar at a marina just outside New York City. He had a mansion not far from where he kept the plane. In less than two hours, he was pulling his Bentley convertible into the garage beneath the Long Island home.

An elevator brought him to the top floor of the three-story mansion and he showered, shaved, and changed into his typical daily uniform: linen slacks, leather sandals, and a heavy cotton shirt.

He grabbed a heavy leaded crystal glass from

the kitchen and splashed some aged whiskey into it and then went to his office. Follett logged onto the computer and waited for the others to arrive.

It didn't take long.

They appeared as video thumbnails on his screen and the audio bogged down with their panic. They were all trying to speak at once and because of the different browser speeds, the result was a garbled mess.

Follett held up his hand and after a few moments everyone became silent.

He already knew they were losing their minds over their partner's death in Brooklyn. There's nothing more permanent than getting one's head blown off and Follett didn't blame them for their fear. But it's what one does with their fear that defines a man.

Once they'd all fallen silent, Follett took command, without the need to rehash what everyone already knew.

"Here's what we're going to do," he began.

CHAPTER FIFTEEN

In the field, a sniper has a spotter. The spotter's job is to help identify targets, judge wind, angle and other factors, and also help the shooter make adjustments in the event a target is missed.

For Rider, he'd worked with a spotter when he was in the military. Once he'd moved on to private work, he'd started working alone and had come to prefer it.

It made sense because the one time he almost died, the closest he'd ever come to cashing in his chips for good, was when his spotter betrayed him.

It had happened in Afghanistan, after he'd alerted his superior office to a problem within the unit. They'd gone out to an area activity north of their base. Something had felt off to Rider, but he hadn't been able to put a finger on it.

When he was in position, his spotter had fallen back slightly.

After a period of time, Rider had gotten into "the zone" and time was relative, he'd realized his spotter hadn't said a word, hadn't recommended adjustments.

Rider looked back.

His spotter was gone.

That's when he heard the bombs falling.

The first impact was so close it felt like his body had been torn apart, but he was still conscious. The second bomb hit, and he didn't remember anything after that.

When he finally came to, he was fighting for his life, surrounded by strangers.

But he survived.

Barely.

With no help from his spotter.

So now, he was working alone and it was as natural to him as anything. However, he wasn't really a solo operation. He had a spotter, in a sense, just not in the field.

Her name was Reese and the incoming call on his burner phone was her number.

"Hey," he said.

"Change of plans," she said.

Rider's hand steadied on the wheel. He didn't like sudden changes as they almost always led to mistakes. And mistakes in his line of work were the kind that meant you never made another one.

"We've got an opportunity back in New York too good to pass up," Reese continued. "It's one we've been waiting for."

"As long as it's not too good to be true," Rider replied.

He heard Reese laugh softly on the other end of the line.

"My job is to identify the targets," she said. "Have I ever steered you wrong?"

"No," Rider said.

But in his mind, he was thinking, *not yet*.

CHAPTER SIXTEEN

Tallon read the text message from his buddy, Brock, about the murder in Brooklyn.

Rather than responding with a text of his own, he called him directly. Secretly, Tallon hated texting and always preferred actual conversation. Especially when it came to something like this.

"What the hell are you up to, Brock?" Tallon asked.

In the background, Tallon thought he could hear a baseball game announcer.

"Just watching the Tigers lose again," Brock said. He was a lifelong Detroiter and always wore a Detroit Tigers baseball cap. Tallon knew Brock could cite statistics for every Tigers team going all the way back to the days of Ty Cobb.

Suddenly, the sound of the baseball game stopped.

"What about you?" Brock asked.

"Just got back from a run."

"Same old Tallon."

Tallon sat back in his leather club chair in the living room and put his feet up on the matching ottoman. It was true; his commitment to fitness had been a bit legendary even among Special Forces. Still, he wasn't that young anymore and he would feel the effects of the run in about a half hour or so. It was the kind of soreness he welcomed.

"So you got my message?" Brock asked.

"Sure did. So how do you know it was an RKN74?"

Brock sighed. "I can't name names but a buddy of mine from Detroit works for NYPD's SWAT team. Apparently, they were talking about this old guy getting nailed by a sniper right there in the middle of Brooklyn. And then the ballistics that came in were super weird – and he remem-bered me telling him about that guy we both sort of knew of."

Tallon smiled inwardly at Brock's reticence to be specific. But he knew exactly what he was talking about. When they'd both been deployed in Afghanistan, they'd heard about a legendary sniper who insisted on using a certain kind of Russian ammunition.

That, in and of itself, wasn't unusual.

What was unusual were the rumors about the sniper himself. People said he was like a ghost and there was speculation he did a lot of work off the books. The kind of work no one wanted to talk about.

"I thought he was dead," Tallon said.

He hadn't thought about the shooter in years because of that: word had spread that the sniper had been killed behind enemy lines on one of those "non-sanctioned" missions. It was the kind of story that often occurred among men like them; lies and whispers were the cornerstone of their occupation. Sometimes, stories just took on lives of their own.

"Maybe he was," Brock replied. His voice betrayed a certain lack of confidence in the statement.

"From what little we know about the guy, this would be right up his alley," Tallon said. Meaning, the guy was mysterious to begin with, a dispute over whether he was actually dead or not would make perfect sense.

"But why an old man in Brooklyn?"

"Maybe it was his ammo, but not him."

Brock scoffed. "Seems strange: a legendary sniper and his custom ammunition are used by another sniper? The guy was a ghost, remember? It's not like he had a bunch of buddies he shared his information with."

Tallon realized he'd forgotten the man's nickname.

"That's right – everyone called him the Ghost," Tallon said.

"Not quite. Ghost Rider was the full handle. But most people shortened it."

"Oh yeah," Tallon said. "Rider."

CHAPTER SEVENTEEN

"She took the bait," Foley said.

He was thin with a ferret-like face, dressed all in black: black nylon parachute pants, black t-shirt and black boots.

Behind him towered a second man dressed all in black.

"About time," the bigger man said.

They both watched a computer terminal with a direct access portal into the Pentagon's system. It was an authorized access. The computer station was in the middle of the room, facing floor-to-ceiling glass windows that gave them a view of the bucolic Virginia countryside. Even though it wasn't visible from this vantage point, the office was located less than five miles from the headquarters of the Central Intelligence Agency.

The big man's name was Jekell. No one knew if that was his real name or a nickname derived from the infamous Jekyll and Hyde story. Most thought it was his real name because the big man did not have any kind of split personality: he was characterized by one overpowering personality characteristic: he lived to destroy.

"Are you sure we need her?" Foley asked, without taking his eyes from the computer screen. His thin, sallow face took on a slightly blue hue from the glow of the screen. It made his pencil-thin moustache look like a digital shadow. "I mean, the NYPD is after him, and now the FBI, too, since he whacked Ortiz. You don't kill a congressman and get away with it."

Jekell's face remained impassive. "You should think before you speak. I don't really care if he gets caught. I care about what he can say if he does. We can't let that happen. It's more important than ever we find him first. So yes, we sure as hell need her."

"Tell me as soon as she takes action, and keep me updated on the Feebies," Jekell ordered.

"Sure," Foley said. "Where will you be if I need to get ahold of you fast?"

The door slammed shut with Jekell's response.

"Okay, then," Foley said to the empty room.

CHAPTER EIGHTEEN

"I've got good news and I've got bad news," Pauling's hacker said over a secure line. It actually wasn't a cell phone – it was a private chat room the hacker, whose name was a rather mundane Dave, had set up. He told Pauling it was the safest way for them to communicate. Rather than relying on a cellular carrier and network, he was in complete control of the feed. Security, he said, was airtight.

"Start with the bad," Pauling said. She was in the safety of her loft but still felt the need to be clandestine.

"Okay."

She studied his small thumbnail video image on her computer screen. He looked exactly like what he was: a middle-aged man who spent most of his time sitting at a desk. He had sandy hair tinged with gray and a plain shirt with a collar. Dave would not have done well in prison, and they both knew it. That might have had something to do with his undying commitment to Pauling.

"The bad news is my visit into the Pentagon's computers did not go unnoticed," he said.

Pauling didn't like the sound of that. It was a pretty serious offense that could result in serious time for both of them. But Dave was the best at what he did and she had a feeling he was about to explain why she shouldn't be worried.

"Here's why you shouldn't be worried," Dave said, on cue. "They know I went in, but they don't know who or where I am. If they were to actually trace my access – it would lead them to a computer in Iceland which was just smashed into pieces and dumped into a glacial lake, thanks to an associate who has no idea who or where I am. It's amazing what you can buy on the Internet."

"Okay, that's better," Pauling said. "The good news?"

"The good news is, I think I found what you were looking for."

A new desktop folder icon appeared miraculously on Pauling's computer screen.

"I literally ran a million different searches with all the variables you mentioned and this is the only thing that came up," Dave said. "When I read it, it seems like the thing you might be looking for. And since it was literally the only single thing I could find, I'm hoping I'm right."

"Okay, thank you, Dave. Let me know how much I owe you." Even though he would have done the work for free, Pauling insisted on paying even though it wasn't on her official books.

A document appeared on Pauling's screen and she knew it was Dave's bill.

"You got it, Pauling. Let me know if you need any more help."

Dave's video image went away and Pauling double-clicked on the folder.

It contained a single document with the heading *Criminal Investigation Command*. Pauling noted the date and the absence of names. The page contained only two paragraphs:

"110th *MP seeking information regarding multiple homicides and civilian abductions north of Mehtar Lam.*"

. . .

Pauling knew FOB stood for Forward Operating Base. Mehtar Lam was certainly a city or region in Afghanistan.

The last paragraph was what had most likely been flagged by Dave's search parameters within the Pentagon's files:

"Seeking information on rogue unit named Grim Reaper as reported by multiple intel sources. Recommend immediate full investigation and full resource allocation. Also recommend highest classification for secured communication."

Pauling read through the paragraphs twice and then looked again at the date.

Knowing Reacher's history, the date was right around the time of his dismissal from the Army.

Had his departure from the military been because of this investigation? Had it triggered his leaving the Army? Or was it merely coincidence?

Pauling didn't believe in luck or bad timing. Things usually happened for a reason.

Now she sat back and pondered the term Grim Reaper. Could someone have labeled Reacher that? Had he killed multiple civilians and then been ejected from the Army and now someone had dug up evidence of the crime?

No way. Not Jack Reacher.

It was something else.

It had to be.

She already knew investigating a multiple homicide in Afghanistan by a rogue unit was going to be next to impossible. Even though now she had more information. She would have to find out where the hell Mehtar Lam was.

And then double-check and see if Reacher had ever spent time there, although she was posi-tive he hadn't: she'd read his file so often that she practically had it memorized. As far as she could tell he'd never been stationed, or worked in, Afghanistan.

This was all she had so far.

Where next?

At first she was at a loss but then like all good answers, the solution was simple. How had she heard of Reacher's link to a crime in the first place? It wasn't through the Army or the CIA.

It had been via her old pal Haskins at the FBI.

Maybe now that Pauling had a location of the crime, Mehtar Lam, she could use Haskins to work the Bureau for any active or former homi-cide cases. Typically, the CIA handled investigations internationally, but sometimes the lines were blurred and it was Haskins who'd delivered the news in the first place.

Pauling sent her friend a message and a suggestion they meet for a drink, if possible. She also asked, ever heard of Mehtar Lam?

Minutes later, Haskins agreed to the drink, but didn't answer her question.

That was okay, Pauling wasn't looking for a response.

It had been a subtle hint for Haskins to look into that location and bring anything she could find to their next meeting.

Pauling hoped her friend had gotten the message.

CHAPTER NINETEEN

The older black man walked from his living room to the kitchen and then stopped in the hallway.

He was out of breath.

At his age, despite the commitment to staying healthy, cardio wasn't his strong suit.

His name was Barnes and he was just under six feet tall. He wore jeans, a Nike dri-fit T-shirt and slippers. His hair was tightly cropped and tinged with silver. His home, a third floor apartment in Queens was the epitome of a man cave: everything was utilitarian and devoid of any feminine touches. Most of the decorations were sports posters. In the living room, homemade shelves carried the burden of thirty-year-old football trophies. Division II.

Barnes had a touch of asthma. His lungs were making a strange sound, sort of like a slow squeak that would disappear and reappear without any kind of rhythm, like a balloon with a slow leak.

It was this goddamned stupid thing he was doing.

He had to keep moving. Sit in the living room, take a seat and then get up again. Hold his cell phone to his ear, even though there was no one on the end of the line. Walk into the kitchen. Turn on the lights. Sit at the table. Go to the fridge, grab a beer.

Go back to the living room.

Ridiculous. His knees hurt and now his back hurt, too. Besides, every time he grabbed a beer he drank and now he had to piss again. He was going to be drunker than a skunk by the time this was all over.

Climb the stairs to his bedroom. Turn on a light. Then turn off the light and go back to the living room.

It was good exercise, but the thing was, he didn't need to exercise. He had prostate cancer and his doctor had told him he would be dead within the year. It was a horrible way to die because he could no longer have sex and for him, that was the only thing he really lived for anymore. Take that away, and he was just a sack of meat holding up some middle-of-the-road clothing, stinking up an apartment he'd paid off years ago.

Still, this was giving him at least some entertainment.

He knew what was going on.

And if it worked, it would be worth the effort.

If it didn't, well, *what the hell did he have to lose?*

CHAPTER TWENTY

Rider was patient. In fact, he doubted there was another person within one hundred square miles who had the sort of self-discipline and willingness to remain still and focused that he possessed.

Having said that, he was slightly annoyed.

Reese had given him the target's information and he'd scouted the location, choosing the rooftop less than a thousand feet away as the ideal spot. It was almost like the location had been perfectly chosen for a sniper.

The location was the easy part.

The problem was the target.

The older black man was staying maddeningly mobile, and seemed to prefer sitting locations that left him behind a wall or pillar through which Rider couldn't shoot.

It was almost like the man was playing peek-a-boo with him.

As Rider waited for the shot, he moved several times, looking for a better vantage point. Each time he modified his own location, he knew it made him vulnerable. It was a bad strategy for a sniper. It was better to lock in and be still, rather than moving around. To be mobile was infantry. He wasn't infantry, he was an assassin.

He thought about what he'd said to Reese: *don't steer me wrong*.

Reese was the best spotter he'd ever had.

When he'd come back in Afghanistan after having been betrayed by his spotter, he'd been taken in by a family. They'd lost one of their sons to the very people Rider had reported. The boy who disappeared had an older sister; her name was Reshawna and in his opium-fueled delirium he'd started calling her Reese. Not only had she nursed him, but she helped smuggle him out of Afghanistan, and later, he'd returned the favor. Together, they'd taken on a shared mission.

He knew she would never betray him.

But something about this target didn't feel right.

His nerves remained calm but his sniper's sixth sense was alive and well.

The damned old black man had just gotten up from his chair and moved once again to the spot in the kitchen hidden in the corner.

Rider took the moment to pull his eye back from the rifle scope.

As he did, he caught the slightest bit of movement to his left.

He glanced over the rooftops, sure it was a flutter of clothes from a clothesline some penny pincher had set up to dry clothes. Electricity on a dryer cost money, after all. Let the wind do the work, and pocket the difference.

Rider looked at the clothesline, but it was still. There was virtually no breeze.

His eyes focused just beyond the clothesline to the next roof, where he saw the top of something. It looked like–

Rider dove just as he saw the silhouette across the rooftops jolt with the kick of a rifle.

Something tore into Rider's left forearm as he rolled onto the asphalt roof.

He had dragged his rifle with him and now, he came to a squat with the rifle held tightly against his right shoulder.

The pain in his arm wasn't bad, even as blood poured from the wound.

He crabbed across the roof to the far corner, making calculations in his mind. He'd already factored various distances and knew that his rifle was set up for about the right distance. The only question was, could he bring his rifle up and get off the shot?

Only one way to find out: he rose in a fluid motion and found the spot just beyond the clothesline.

It was empty.

Time to go, Rider thought as he raced for the stairwell.

CHAPTER TWENTY-ONE

"Shit!" Follett shouted at the computer screen.

He had landed Peregrine and handed it over to his team at the marina. Now, he was in his home office, staring at a computer screen. He still wore his linen slacks, sandals and cotton shirt but all that was forgotten as he roared at the video playing before him.

The sniper on the roof across from Rider had clearly missed. The GoPro camera mounted on the man's head had given Follett a beautiful view of the whole thing. The camera had live streamed the action straight back to Follett so he could watch his old friend Rider die a most poetic death: shot in the head by a sniper.

Follett and his team had so perfectly set up

the old black man as a decoy, told him to keep moving back and forth, to not give anyone a clear shot.

In the meantime, they'd positioned their own shooter three buildings away, strategically positioned to focus on the only vantage point a qualified sniper would utilize.

And now, their shooter had missed.

Follett got to his feet.

He went to his gun safe and made a selection.

Then, he went to another bedroom – the mansion had no fewer than eight of them.

He opened the door and smiled at the Afghani woman tied to the chair. She was beautiful, even though she had a gag in her mouth and her face was badly bruised. Follett was not aroused by any of it.

It had taken a lot of work to find her, and a lot of money in bribes, but it had worked. The problem was, finding her was always going to be much easier than finding Rider.

"Oh, Reese," Follett said to the woman. "This just isn't your lucky day."

CHAPTER TWENTY-TWO

Rider flew down the stairs, his boots clanging on the metal. He had his rifle slung across his shoulder and a 9mm pistol in his right hand.

The bullet had simply seared his left forearm. No real damage had been done. He'd been lucky.

Very lucky.

Now, he burst through the door into the alley behind the building and raced around the corner. His rental car was parked in a spot in front of a deli and he'd probably gone over the meter, waiting for his shot. That was bad form; a parking ticket was proof that you had been at a certain place at a certain point of time.

As he ran, he knew all along he'd been set up.

Compromised.

The black man had purposely kept moving to keep him waiting for the shot, all while they'd set up their own.

Damnit, he thought.

He had to get word to Reese.

If he was blown, she was too.

He saw his car ahead just as shots rang out and bullets clipped the brickwork next to his head. Bits of broken stone tore into his face and he saw the shooter on his left. The man had probably descended from the rooftop where he'd taken his shot at Rider.

The timing made sense.

Anger burned inside Rider and he was determined to make it out of the mission alive.

Rider fired as he ran and the man ducked down. Rider made it to his car, threw his rifle inside and saw another blur of movement in his peripheral vision.

The man had ducked around a parked car and was aiming a pistol at Rider.

Rider did the opposite of what the man expected: rather than slide further into the car in order to start it and escape, he sprang outward, away from the steering wheel.

It was classic sniper strategy: put yourself where they won't expect you.

The man's shot blew apart the side view mirror, missing Rider by at least two feet.

Rider aimed carefully and fired twice, a double tap, and saw his bullets blow apart the man's head. The body fell to the curb, slack.

It wasn't the most elegant kill, but definitely one of the more satisfying, Rider thought.

He was tempted to run across and look for identification on the dead man but it didn't matter. He knew who they were. Rider needed to get the hell out of there; sirens were already getting louder and he had to call Reese.

Assuming she was still alive.

Behind the wheel, he threw the car into gear and drove fast, putting ten city blocks behind him before he fished out his cell phone.

He dialed Reese and waited, his breath slowly going back to normal.

On the third ring, his call was answered.

"Hello Rider," a voice said. "Reese can't come to the phone right now because...she's dead."

Rider listened to the man laugh and he recognized Follett's voice.

"You're a dead man walking," Rider said.

He disconnected the call and broke the phone into pieces, tossing them out of the car as he drove.

CHAPTER TWENTY-THREE

Tallon studied the mountain lion through his spotting scope. He could see the big cat was starving; his ribs were visible and he looked gaunt.

Tallon brought the rifle to his shoulder, aimed, and fired.

The cat flopped onto its side.

Even for Death Valley it was hot; over one hundred degrees and not an ounce of breeze. It was late afternoon, the sun was still high overhead and even the birds were somewhere in the shade. The sky was nothing but pure blue, designed to make the heat as intense as possible.

Tallon jogged ahead and studied the fallen animal. He was still breathing. Tallon had fired a tranquilizer and now, the cat was knocked out.

Tallon could see the mountain lion's broken leg. It was infected. Tallon traced a line of green all the way from the break into the big predator's chest. No wonder the mountain lion had followed him; he was dying, and he probably knew it.

There was no chance he could take the cat back to a vet in his little town; the infection would be too far gone. Froth on the cat's mouth was the telltale sign.

With a heavy heart, Tallon placed the muzzle of his pistol against the cat's head and fired.

It was the only way.

He walked back to his ranch and cleaned the pistol. His cell phone vibrated and he checked the screen.

It was his buddy Brock.

This time the message was a bit longer.

Ever hear of Jack Reacher? He has something to do with our buddy.

Tallon frowned.

Reacher?

The name didn't mean much to him, but Pauling had told him about the dude: an Army MP who kicked ass everywhere he went. Tallon's kind of guy.

What did Reacher have to do with the sniper he and Brock knew from Afghanistan?

Tallon hit the "Favorites" button on his phone and saw Pauling's number.

He tapped it.

He was going to call her anyway, now he had a question for her.

CHAPTER TWENTY-FOUR

Detective Claire Brewster whistled at the contents of Victor Panko's computer. The tech guys had finally broken through the complicated encryption on the old man's desktop.

For a man who worked for a charity, he was big on secrecy.

The team had found a cache of child pornography: thousands of images and videos that made Claire sick to her stomach.

The charity, she found out, was supposedly an orphanage in Afghanistan.

But what Claire and her team soon discovered was that the orphanage didn't exist. There was no physical structure – they'd used aerial photography and images from the military to scour the area.

There was nothing but a small village, ravaged by war and the opium trade.

Clearly, the orphanage was really just a pipe-line of young children from a war-torn country delivered directly to pedophiles.

Mostly in the US.

Claire had read the names with great interest. They were listed as individuals who'd filed for "adoption." In most cases, the names were fake as were the phone numbers and addresses. But a member of the team had discovered the cypher and broken down the code.

Real names and real numbers had appeared before them.

One of the list of Americans welcoming young, pre-adolescent boys into the US: the recently deceased Congressman Ortiz.

Claire realized she was in the middle of some-thing much bigger than she'd first thought.

A ring of pedophiles.

Which was certainly a crime in and of itself.

More interesting, however, was the ensuing crime that had brought the ring to her attention in the first place.

Someone was killing them.

One shot at a time.

CHAPTER TWENTY-FIVE

The bar was called the Double Olive and it was a martini bar in central Manhattan. Pauling arrived first and ordered a dirty martini with a blue cheese stuffed olive. It was clearly the after-work crowd: lots of ties loosened, voices getting progressively louder and corporate angst being relieved.

It was a ritual Pauling had experienced firsthand.

A man on the other end of the bar was getting ready to approach Pauling. He'd been making obvious eye contact, and had chugged his last drink for courage, when, thankfully, Haskins arrived.

She slid onto the stool next to Pauling and they gave each other a quick hug.

Pauling was surprised to smell the scent of alcohol on Haskins.

Had she stopped somewhere else first?

Haskins ordered a dry martini and when it came they clinked glasses.

"So much better than espresso," Pauling joked.

"I can't argue with that," Haskins replied.

"How was work?" Pauling asked, wondering if her friend was slurring her words slightly. If so, that was a very bad sign.

"Busy, busy, busy," Haskins said. "This Russian oligarch is into all kinds of shit. How about you?"

"I'm tied up on this Reacher thing," Pauling said. For the time being, she wasn't going to confront Haskins on what was potentially an issue. "Turns out, there was an investigation in Afghanistan, but I don't think Reacher was involved because it was just after he'd left the Army. Still, this whole notion of a unit called the Grim Reaper seems over the top, even for war time. Were you able to find out anything?"

Haskins looked aside.

"What's wrong?" Pauling asked.

Her friend's hand shook as she picked up her martini.

"I'm going to tell you something but you have

to swear you won't tell anyone else. I'll deny it to my dying breath."

"Okay," Pauling said. She studied her friend: her eyes were wide and slightly bloodshot.

"I've got a problem," Haskins said. "And someone knows about it, and they asked me to mention the Reacher thing to you. And they also said if you asked about this case, I was supposed to give you this."

Haskins withdrew an envelope from her soft leather briefcase, folded in half.

"It's the investigation you were asking about," Haskins said. "I don't know if it's true or not, but it has to do with an Army officer named Brad Follett. A bad guy. And...and, I've got a problem but my friendship with you is more important."

Haskins was about to start crying and Pauling wanted to comfort her friend.

"But why?"

"I don't know. All I know is I looked up this Follett guy and he's a dangerous man. You need to be careful."

Haskins drank the rest of her martini in one gulp.

"I've got to go," she said.

"No," Pauling said. "Let me–"

"If I say anything else I'll be in trouble."

She put a hand on Pauling's wrist. The hand was ice cold.

"I'm sorry, Lauren. I need help. But not now."

Haskins left and Pauling watched her go, as guilt consumed her. She would have to find a way to help her friend. Whatever it took, she would do it.

But in the meantime, she had to clear Reacher's name.

She opened the envelope and read about Brad Follett.

When the man on the other end of the bar approached her, she didn't even look up as he arrived.

She simply said, "Go away, please, I'm working."

The man slunk back to his corner of the bar and asked for the check. He was one and done.

Pauling began to read and then her phone rang.

"Hey Tallon," she said, seeing his name on her phone screen.

She listened to him explain about the sniper, ballistics, and finally, Reacher's name.

Pauling never believed in coincidences.

"How soon can you get here?" she asked.

CHAPTER TWENTY-SIX

Rider drove straight to Reese's place, even though he suspected she was dead. From a purely tactical standpoint, however, he believed that she wouldn't have been killed in her home.

He had stopped at a drug store, bought antiseptic and bandages, and stitched up his forearm. The bullet had literally ripped apart his tattoo: a skull breathing fire. It was meant to represent his nickname: the Ghost Rider. He'd gotten it when he was a very young man and always thought about getting it removed.

How appropriate that his enemies had partially taken care of the job for him.

He was fine. He would live and that was all that mattered.

Rider no longer felt any sense of accomplishment or satisfaction. What burned within him now was rage.

As pure and crystalline as the freshly driven snow.

He couldn't stop thinking about the time when he'd been an altar boy in his innocent little hometown and the priest had taken him back into his private quarters after mass. He'd done things to Rider that he simply hadn't understood until much later.

When he had, he'd tracked the priest down and killed him. That had been pretty simple.

Until the shit in Afghanistan had exploded.

And then Reese had saved him.

An angel who'd brought him back to life. More than that, she'd shown him his new mission: to make the men who preyed on the innocent pay.

Rider hung his head.

Now, Reese was dead.

He pulled his rental car up to her apartment building and used a lock pick to get inside. She lived in a modest area of Tribeca. A bit bohemian, perhaps, but full of energy and ideas.

Just like Reese herself.

Once inside, he could see there had been a

struggle. He and Reese had never consummated their relationship, but they'd spent time together. Rider knew the apartment, knew where things belonged.

He thought about Reese and her love of music, food, and life.

But now, there was nothing.

Rider went into her bedroom and looked at her desktop computer. He pulled the keyboard to him, booted it up and saw that it had been wiped clean. The desktop was a blank screen.

He searched 'recent documents' and saw no history. Someone had been very, very thorough.

But Rider knew Reese very well. He found a remote hard drive at the top of her closet. He plugged it into the computer and saw that it contained recordings of the cameras from the apartment.

When the man stepped in, Rider knew him instantly.

Follett.

The sight of the man set his jaw on edge. He ground his teeth and felt blood rage at a level he'd never experienced.

Rider went down to the apartment building's security center and asked to see video of anyone in the parking garage or the street from the last twenty-four hours. Along with the request, he provided a hundred-dollar bill.

Now that he had full cooperation, Rider learned that a street camera guarding the entrance recorded a Range Rover cruising past. Not once. But three times.

There was a visible license plate.

Rider jotted down the plate number and sent a message to a former special ops guy who now worked at the NYPD.

Moments later an address popped up on Rider's phone.

Follett, Rider thought. *Finally*.

Rider got back into his rental car and headed out to Long Island.

CHAPTER TWENTY-SEVEN

The first flight from Las Vegas, the airport nearest Tallon, brought him into New York just before midnight.

He Ubered to Pauling's place and rang the bell.

As he waited for her to buzz him in, a black Cadillac Escalade passed down the street.

Tallon paid it no mind.

Pauling buzzed him in and he took the elevator to her loft.

When she opened the door, he stepped in and kissed her, then licked her lips.

"Mmm," he said. "Have you been drinking gin?"

"Excellent sense of taste," she said. "Yeah, I

had a martini earlier. It's good to see you, by the way."

They bypassed any more discussion and went immediately to the bedroom.

An hour later, they returned to the kitchen and grabbed some leftovers from the fridge, a glass of wine for Pauling, and a beer for Tallon.

"So tell me," Tallon said. "What the hell is going on?"

CHAPTER TWENTY-EIGHT

Jekell parked the Escalade down the street from Pauling's loft.

He checked his pistol – a Glock 10mm and made sure it was loaded. Jekell wasn't an idiot, he knew Pauling's background, as well as Tallon's. He wasn't about to perform a full frontal assault.

That wasn't the point.

In a sense, they were working for him.

Like the very sniper he was pursuing, Jekell just had to be patient. He would let Tallon and Pauling have a short amount of time together, and then they would lead him to the man he pursued.

And then Jekell would kill that man.

If necessary, he would kill Tallon and Pauling too.

Jekell felt no warmth or psychopathic need.

It was just business.

The fact was, the best secrets were buried deep.

And if someone showed up with a shovel, well, they would need to be buried as well.

CHAPTER TWENTY-NINE

Tallon and Pauling pored over the file from Haskins.

"So let me get this straight," Pauling said. "Brad Follett was the CO of a special ops team in Afghanistan. At some point, and there is no official explanation why, the group was disbanded."

Tallon nodded. "Happens all the time," he said. "When there's a problem in a unit, whether it's bad morale, or more often, poor leadership, they basically break the team up and redistribute the individual pieces. If the individuals turn things around, it's usually a sign leadership was bad. Meaning, the issue was systemic and everyone gets a new lease on life, so to speak."

"So it would make sense if Follett fell off the radar after this," Pauling said. It wasn't a statement, more of a question.

"Not really," Tallon said. "The military is usually pretty good at keeping track of people, as long as they're in the service. Once they're out, you can keep tabs on them through their finances – if they're still receiving pay or benefits. If not, only then do they disappear. Off the grid, so to speak – but only if they go all the way."

Pauling studied the thin file.

"Or change their identity."

Tallon nodded. "That, too."

Pauling found nothing in the file. There wasn't much else to go on, other than a single incident report.

"What about this field report about a member of the team who went missing in action? A sniper."

Tallon had noticed that, too.

"It's odd because I was just talking about a sniper in Afghanistan. A legendary guy, really who used a special kind of Russian ammunition called RKN74," Tallon said. "He disappeared. Presumed dead. It wasn't unheard of, at the time."

Pauling studied Tallon's face. "I don't believe

in coincidences." She filled him in on how Haskins had been coerced into getting Pauling involved. "How well do you know your buddy?"

"Brock?" Tallon shrugged. "Pretty well, I guess. When he mentioned Reacher, I thought it was a bit odd."

Tallon picked up the phone and dialed Brock's number. "Hey, how did you come across Reacher's name?" he asked.

Pauling watched as Tallon's eyes narrowed.

"In a text message."

Tallon glanced over at Pauling.

"Okay, roger that."

Tallon hung up.

"Brock says he never sent me a text message about Reacher." Tallon held up his phone. "But it's right here."

Pauling nodded. "Okay, that's some high-tech spook stuff right there. The ability to hijack a phone?"

Tallon nodded. He studied the file.

"Where did this Grim Reaper handle come from?" he asked.

"It was first mentioned in this Army investigation file I got from the Pentagon," Pauling said. "Why?"

"Because the initials G and R make me

curious."

"Tell me more."

"Because the missing sniper? His handle was Ghost Rider."

"That's strange," Pauling said. "What was his real name?"

"Joe. Joe Rider."

Pauling looked back at the file. "It makes sense. He would have been in that unit."

Tallon nodded. "Brad Follett would have been his CO."

"We need to talk to him," Pauling said. "If Follett was the CO, he would have been at the center of the investigation. He would know if Reacher had been involved, if at all. And while we're at it, maybe we can figure out what the hell really happened to Joe Rider."

Tallon wasn't convinced. "I just don't understand if Rider didn't die in Afghanistan, why did he come back and shoot an old guy in Brooklyn?"

Pauling realized she hadn't brought Tallon up to speed on the ballistics. "You heard about the murder of Congressman Ortiz?"

"Yes," Tallon said. "Oh no..."

"Yeah, those ballistics were the same as the old guy in Brooklyn. Same shooter."

"Shit," Tallon said. "We've got to find Follett, and fast."

Pauling held up her phone.

"I'm pulling some strings with my old company. Let's go."

CHAPTER THIRTY

Rider knew he was playing his end game.

When he'd discovered, back in Afghanistan, that Follett was possibly involved in the disappearances of some of the young children, all boys, in the villages they were supposedly protecting, he broke his sniper's silence. There were very few secrets among men fighting side by side in a place like Afghanistan, and word got out quickly.

Rider still wasn't sure how they got to his spotter so quickly and turned him, but they did.

The ambush happened, air support given his coordinates: people died by friendly fire all the time. What was one more dead sniper in the barren mountains of some godforsaken country halfway around the world?

Rider had slowly recovered thanks to Reese and her family, even as Follett's cronies desperately searched for his body. It took him nearly six months to be able to walk again and when he was able to travel, he learned that Follett's unit had been disbanded and his old CO was gone.

Eventually, Rider made it back to the States where he'd gone underground, before rejoining Reese, and creating their new mission.

Together, they'd made the decision to take down Follett's pedophile ring, and hopefully find Follett himself. He'd disappeared since leaving the military, abruptly.

And no one knew where to find him.

Until now.

Rider followed his phone's navigation to a prestigious area of Long Island and pulled around the block from a stunning, contemporary home with an ocean view. He knew Follett loved seaplanes and probably had a hangar somewhere around here.

It was classic Follett, he knew. Showy. Private. But most of all: it was strategic. The home was at the top of a slight rise that sloped down toward the ocean.

Even in hiding, Follett had taken up the position on high ground.

Rider parked his car, double-checked his weapons and circled back to the house.

He weighed his options. Follett would certainly have a top-of-the-line security system, complete with all the bells and whistles like video, motion sensors, maybe even infrared.

At the same time, Follett was no fool. He would know that Rider was on his way, it was why he'd taunted him over the phone. Follett wanted Rider here, to lure him in and kill him once and for all.

Rider was sure Follett intended to finish the job he'd tried to accomplish back in Afghanistan.

The safest play to begin with was the direct approach: Rider went to the front door and found it unlocked.

He smiled.

How nice of Follett to make him feel right at home.

Rider opened the door and stepped inside.

CHAPTER THIRTY-ONE

D etective Claire Brewster had her car's strobe lights flashing as she raced toward Long Island. New Yorkers hated to get out of the way and pretended they had nowhere to go. Claire had no patience with them; she rode their bumpers and jammed herself between vehicles, wishing she could return and ticket all of them for failure to comply.

Things were rocketing ahead faster than Claire had expected: she'd had a warrant assigned to her by a friendly judge, and now she, along with a crash team specifically trained to take down armed fugitives, were headed for the residence of one Brad Follett.

His name had appeared in Victor Panko's

computer files, although it had taken some serious digging by the NYPD's cyber crime division. Not only was Follett's real name eventually discovered, it appeared as if he was the de facto head of the sick little group.

Financial investigators had even tracked down a seaplane in a private hangar that belonged to Follett, who was a licensed pilot. Claire had some theories about why a pedophile and possible psychopath like Follett might want his own plane and the ability to travel incognito, to a certain degree.

If there was one thing in common with sex criminals, they all had a mania for extreme privacy, for obvious reasons.

Claire still wasn't sure who was behind the killing of Panko and Ortiz, but she had a feeling Follett would be at the top of their list and she wanted to get to him before this sniper did.

A bullet to the head, while Follett certainly deserved it, was too easy. Too quick. Claire wanted this Follett guy to be put on trial, to answer to his crimes for all the young lives he'd ruined. He'd taken advantage of wartime orphans, sold them into sex slavery and apparently had a good time doing it.

It had certainly been profitable.

She'd taken a look at the Long Island mansion that matched Follett's address and whistled. It was worth at least a couple million.

Claire wondered if the sniper was already in position.

CHAPTER THIRTY-TWO

Pauling pulled her Mercedes SUV out of the underground parking garage and headed for Long Island. She'd just gotten the address from her old firm's best skip tracer; armed with the new information they'd gotten on Follett, including service record and social security number, linking him to a physical address took her former colleague less than twenty minutes.

As she drove, Pauling didn't notice the black SUV three cars behind her.

"So what do you think happened? Was it another My Lai?" Pauling asked. They still hadn't been able to discover what crime had taken place under Follett's command.

Tallon shook his head. "Not in this day and age," he replied, in response to the idea of a civilian massacre like the one that had happened in Vietnam so many decades ago. Tallon knew My Lai was still used as an educational and training tool – as a perfect example of how failure of leadership can lead to horrific behavior by soldiers.

"Too many cell phones with audio and video," Tallon continued. "I'm not saying it can't happen, but things have changed. So much of warfare now is conducted out in the open, and I'm not talking guns and bombs. I'm talking public relations. Do you remember when that soldier draped an American flag over the fallen statue of Saddam Hussein? All hell broke loose."

"Yeah, the narrative is as important as the war."

They both rode in silence.

"Then what do you think happened?" Pauling asked. "Afghanistan is full of heroin – maybe they were involved in drug dealing. Shipping stuff back home. Or maybe murder on a smaller level. What if this Joe Rider went crazy and shot a bunch of people?"

"It's certainly possible," Tallon said. "But it doesn't fit for me. From what I'd heard Rider was a true sniper: dedicated. A ghost. Serious about his profession. Guys like that usually don't go off the deep end."

"No? What about the old man in Brooklyn and Congressman Ortiz?"

Tallon looked out the windows as they left the city. "I don't have an answer for that. All I can tell you is the guys who usually go off the deep end are the undisciplined ones who get sloppy and careless and have serious, underlying issues," he said. "If anything, a guy like Rider might have witnessed something he shouldn't have, and someone disappeared him."

"Now that makes way more sense."

"But if it was Rider who's been shooting civilians back here..."

The unspoken thought hung in the air.

"Maybe Follett can shed some light on all of this," Pauling said.

"Maybe," Tallon said. He was looking at his side view mirror. There had been a black SUV behind them, but now, it was gone.

"Here we are," Pauling said as she pulled up to the house. There were no cars in the driveway and no obvious signs someone was home.

There were sirens in the distance.

"Locked and loaded?" Tallon asked her.

"Let's go," she said and headed for the front door.

CHAPTER THIRTY-THREE

During his time in active service, Follett wasn't a sniper. He was a crack shot with both a rifle and a pistol, but the long gun hadn't been his primary weapon.

As a CO, snipers had been under his command and he had worked closely with many of them in the field, including Joe Rider.

Rider was the best he'd ever seen.

A ghost.

The problem was, Rider was also one of those holier-than-thou kind of guys. Always pretending to think of others, there to save the world.

It was all bullshit, Follett thought. The only thing that mattered in this life was getting yours before you died. It didn't matter what you wanted, but what was the point of helping others?

When you died, no one would remember the good things you'd done.

Follett had spent his life acquiring things he desired, be it young boys, fancy toys or ocean-front property. That guiding desire had never done him wrong.

And right now, all he wanted was to put a bullet through Joe Rider's head. Follett had suspected back in Afghanistan that the ambush hadn't been successful. But the Ghost had slipped away.

Well, he wouldn't make the same mistake twice.

Snipers were all about precision, patience and camouflage. Follett also had the advantage of firsthand knowledge of the battlefield; it was his home after all. When he had taunted Rider after killing the Afghani girl, Follett knew the sniper would track him down and try to kill him.

Follett utilized his familiarity with the house and it's L-shape, designed to maximize ocean views from every room. His master bedroom included a balcony at one end of the L that provided an overhang with a full view of the great room.

Follett had chosen his own rifle, chambered with Rider's favorite RKN74 ammo as a bit of poetic justice. Nothing in his life was ever done without first thinking how to maximize pleasure from the action.

He'd already seen a shadow in the great room and knew it was Rider. This was because his home alarm system included a video feed linked directly to his phone. So he'd been able to see Rider enter the house.

Now, Follett was tempted to check his phone but he didn't want to miss his shot, either.

The key was the kitchen. It sported a huge breakfast bar and anyone entering the home looking to kill its owner would certainly approach the marble-topped partition and look behind it. When Rider did that, Follett would blow his head off.

He just had to be patient.

CHAPTER THIRTY-FOUR

H*igh ground.*

Rider weighed what he knew of Follett and the layout of the house. He also knew that Follett's ego was about the same size as this Long Island mansion, maybe even a little larger.

He would want to beat Rider at his own game.

Which meant most likely that Follett had taken the high ground. When he'd driven past, Rider had noted the angles of the house, the overall L-shape designed to give views from every window, along with various porches and balconies, particularly the one on the south end of the house.

The security cameras were visible, too. So when he entered, Rider had gone straight away from the kitchen to a mud room. It consisted of a short hallway with rows of cubbies on the left, and hooks for coats on the right. The hooks were empty, as were the shelves.

It didn't look like Follett spent a lot of time at the house.

Rider stopped short of actually entering the space, though, because there was a camera trained at the back door. It was positioned in the corner of the hall's doorway, which meant its blind spot ended a few feet into the room.

It was why Rider had stopped as he was now just behind the camera. He simply pulled out his short folding knife, reached up and neatly sliced the cable at the rear of the camera.

And then he walked out the back door.

He quickly circled around the house until he reached the corner of the southern end of the L.

Rider dropped to the ground with his rifle in hand. He slowly pulled himself along the wet grass until he could just see the edge of the balcony.

What he saw was a gift: Follett was prone on the deck of the balcony, looking down into the great room.

Rider brought his rifle to his shoulder.

The balcony was made of plank decking, with

a modern railing. A patch of Follett's head was just visible through two rows of the railing's cables.

Rider heard sirens and could see through the great room window that someone else was coming through the front door.

He had to take the shot, and take it now.

Rider's finger tightened on the trigger.

He put the crosshairs on the back of Follett's head.

He let out an easy breath, slowly squeezed the trigger and then everything went black.

CHAPTER THIRTY-FIVE

Pauling heard the sound of two gunshots coming from behind the house. She was already inside, heading for the kitchen, but Tallon had circled to the back.

She turned to run and provide cover for Tallon, but saw through the window as a stream of police cars roared into the driveway.

A woman emerged from the first car – an unmarked with lights flashing from the car's grill. A detective, no doubt.

From behind her, a group of cops fanned out, all wearing blue jackets and bulletproof vests.

They would get to Tallon before she could.

Pauling put her pistol on the kitchen counter and stepped outside with her hands in the air.

A third gunshot sounded.

Tallon, she thought.

CHAPTER THIRTY-SIX

For a big man, Jekell moved with the kind of physical grace that had served him well over the years. People never expected a man of his size could be so light on his feet.

He'd parked the black Escalade on the other side of the Long Island mansion, after seeing Pauling and Tallon park to the west. Then, he'd been able to slip into the backyard just as he saw Rider come through the house's back door.

Jekell hadn't moved a muscle, not even a twitch.

He knew all too well what Rider was capable of.

It had been Jekell's job to make Rider disappear back in Afghanistan, and he'd failed. As a private contractor frequently employed by the CIA, it was the only blemish on his resumé.

Jekell had never lost to anyone in the field, and he'd made it his mission to track down Rider. He had no idea why anyone had wanted the man killed in the first place, but as long as the sniper was still loose, Jekell's credibility to clients was shattered.

It was why he'd put together a plan: find the original investigator who'd worked the case. The name Jack Reacher had come up, but no one could find him. However, a former FBI agent turned private investigator had ties to Reacher. And, she worked frequently with a former special ops soldier named Michael Tallon.

They'd been the perfect team for Jekell to exploit.

And now, finally, he had Rider in his crosshairs, not the other way around.

Jekell watched the sniper go to the ground and slowly bring his rifle to bear.

At last, Jekell moved and walked slowly toward Rider, his Glock aimed at the man's head. He could tell Rider was about to fire.

Jekell's finger tightened on the trigger and just as he fired, Rider fired, too.

CHAPTER THIRTY-SEVEN

Tallon's years in combat provided him the ability to take in information rapidly and process it with reflex-like speed.

He'd come around the corner of the house after exiting the back door and saw two things simultaneously: the black Cadillac Escalade he'd seen behind them on the highway, and now, a man dressed in black with a pistol in his hand.

Tallon noted the Glock, the tension in the man's body and knew he was about to fire. The target wasn't visible, as the man was aiming at something around the corner of the house.

The man fired.

Tallon saw the big man's wrists flex with the

recoil and then with shocking quickness and in a fluid motion, he wheeled on Tallon.

"No," Tallon said. His own gun was in his hand as the man's gun came in line.

Everything slowed down for Tallon. The man had followed them. He'd been after the same quarry, which meant the shooter now facing him had planned to deal with he and Pauling.

It all raced through Tallon's mind with breath-taking clarity. They'd been used to flush out the game.

And now, the man was going to retire them, too.

The big man's gun didn't waver and a small smile tugged at the corner of his mouth.

"Put it down," Tallon said.

But the man's finger tightened on the trigger, so Tallon fired three times fast, all center mass.

The big man got off one shot that crashed into a window somewhere behind Tallon's head.

It seemed to happen in slow motion: the big man took a slight step forward, the gun fell from his hands and then he slowly fell forward, crashing face first into the ground.

Tallon knew he was dead before he hit the ground.

Suddenly, there were a half-dozen cops in

matching blue windbreakers fanning out around Tallon.

"Put it down," they said.

Unlike the dead man on the ground, Tallon followed orders.

CHAPTER THIRTY-EIGHT

D etective Claire Brewster stood next to Pauling and Tallon. They were both in handcuffs although Claire had verified they were, in fact, who they said they were. She didn't care much for private investigators and right now, they were the least of her concerns.

They stood over the big, dead man dressed all in black. The home's owner, Brad Follett, also deceased, had already been identified.

"Who is he?" Tallon asked, lifting his chin toward the dead man.

Brewster looked back at him. "How the hell should I know? You're the one who killed him."

Tallon had to admit, she had a point.

Together, they walked to the edge of the

house and Tallon saw a pool of blood on the grass. A rifle lay next to the blood.

But there was no body.

Tallon glanced at Pauling who nodded back at him.

Rider.

The Ghost.

He'd done it again.

CHAPTER THIRTY-NINE

They spent nearly a full day in an interrogation room in the bowels of the NYPD before Pauling's attorney finally sprung them both.

There were no pending charges against Tallon, as the shooting was clearly in self-defense. Follett's security system also had a camera covering the rear of the property and they'd all been able to see the man now identified as Steven Jekell refuse to comply.

The detective, Brewster, had finally told them off the record, of course, that Jekell had been an ex-CIA operative with a fairly long rap sheet. In fact, there was more than one current investigation into his team for their work overseas.

However, those probes hadn't resulted in any

kind of restrictions on his access to the DOD's technology. Once his identity had been verified, Brewster's team had gone to an office in Virginia where they'd arrested a colleague of Jekell's named Foley, and confiscated all of their computers, weapons and equipment. It had clearly been a black-ops unit, with ties to multiple international incidents.

"He was no doubt involved in the ambush that tried to kill Rider in the first place," Pauling said.

"Guys like him would consider it a stain on his record," Tallon pointed out. "Unfinished business that probably gnawed at him and maybe even cost him contracts. Money and pride to a guy like Jekell are everything."

Claire sipped from a Styrofoam cup of coffee. "He's small potatoes. Follett is the real deal. I wish this Rider guy hadn't blown his head off, because it would have been good to interrogate him. But we're getting loads of evidence, mostly from his plane."

"His plane?" Pauling asked.

"Yeah," Claire replied. "Follett liked to do most of his dirty work in a seaplane. Flying around anonymously, parking in the middle of the ocean somewhere in order to do his dirty work in private."

"Great place to dispose of bodies, too," Tallon said.

"We've got video," Claire said. "Makes you sick to see."

Pauling's attorney waved them toward the door.

"I wonder where Rider is now," Pauling said, ignoring the gesture. She kind of liked this Claire Brewster. The woman seemed like a straight shooter.

Tallon shrugged his shoulders.

"We have no idea, at the moment," Claire said. "I still have no idea how the hell he slipped through our fingers. There was maybe a ten-second window..."

"That's all a guy like Rider needs," Tallon said.

Steam from Claire's coffee rose into the air and disappeared.

CHAPTER FORTY

Rider looked at himself in the mirror.

It wasn't a pretty sight.

The bullet from Jekell's pistol had plowed its way across his forehead before careening off his skull. Now, there was a three-inch gash in his forehead and a chunk of flesh missing. The area around it was swollen and bruised.

It was ugly.

But at least he was still alive.

Rider knew he had his rifle to thank for that. Once again, it had saved his life.

The RKN74 round was a powerful bullet. Even with his custom-fitted rifle the recoil was impressive. When he fired the shot that blew apart Follett's head, the kick from his rifle jolted his head and shoulder back an inch or two.

The beauty of it all was that he, Rider, must have fired a hare's breath before Jekell pulled the trigger.

While Rider's shot found its intended target with deadly accuracy, Jekell's was off by a matter of inches because Rider's head jerked backward.

If Jekell had fired a moment earlier, the bullet probably would have hit him square in the side of the head and it would have been the end of him.

Death by head shot.

Instead, the bullet had slammed along the top of his forehead, peeling off a chunk of flesh and momentarily knocking him unconscious.

When he'd come to an instant later, he'd done what always came naturally: he simply disappeared into the trees separating Follett's house from his neighbors. From there, he'd worked backward, using his sniper's gift of camouflage to eventually leave Long Island.

Now, in the cheap hotel room he studied the gash on his forehead. He thought of Reese and how happy she would be that he'd been able to fulfill their mission. The man who'd been responsible for tearing the life and soul out of her village was finally dead.

Justice, delivered RKN74 style.

Rider winced as he doused his wound with antiseptic. There would be a scar for certain and it wouldn't be pretty.

That was okay, he reasoned.

To most people, he was practically invisible.

BUY THE NEXT BOOK IN THE SERIES

Book #16 in The JACK REACHER Cases

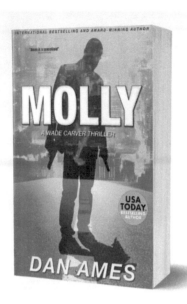

AN AWARD-WINNING BESTSELLING MYSTERY SERIES

Buy DEAD WOOD, the first John Rockne Mystery.

"Fast-paced, engaging, original."

-NY Times bestselling author Thomas Perry

ABOUT THE AUTHOR

Dan Ames is a USA TODAY Bestselling Author, Amazon Kindle #1 bestseller, GoodReads Readers Choice finalist and winner of the Independent Book Award for Crime Fiction.

www.authordanames.com
dan@authordanames.com

ALSO BY DAN AMES

THE JACK REACHER CASES

The JACK REACHER Cases #1 (A Hard Man To Forget)

The JACK REACHER Cases #2 (The Right Man For Revenge)

The JACK REACHER Cases #3 (A Man Made For Killing)

The JACK REACHER Cases #4 (The Last Man To Murder)

The JACK REACHER Cases #5 (The Man With No Mercy)

The JACK REACHER Cases #6 (A Man Out For Blood)

The JACK REACHER Cases #7 (A Man Beyond The Law)

The JACK REACHER Cases #8 (The Man Who Walks Away)

The JACK REACHER Cases (The Man Who Strikes Fear)

The JACK REACHER Cases (The Man Who Stands Tall)

The JACK REACHER Cases (The Man Who Works Alone)

The Jack Reacher Cases (A Man Built For Justice)

The JACK REACHER Cases #13 (A Man Born for Battle)

The JACK REACHER Cases #14 (The Perfect Man for Payback)

The JACK REACHER Cases #15 (The Man Whose Aim Is True)

The JACK REACHER Cases #16 (The Man Who Dies Here)

The JACK REACHER Cases #17 (The Man With Nothing To Lose)

The JACK REACHER Cases #18 (The Man Who Never Goes Back)

The JACK REACHER Cases #19 (The Man From The Shadows)

The JACK REACHER CASES #20 (The Man Behind The Gun)

JACK REACHER'S SPECIAL INVESTIGATORS

BOOK ONE: DEAD MEN WALKING

BOOK TWO: GAME OVER

BOOK THREE: LIGHTS OUT

BOOK FOUR: NEVER FORGIVE, NEVER
FORGET

BOOK FIVE: HIT THEM FAST, HIT
THEM HARD

BOOK SIX: FINISH THE FIGHT

THE JOHN ROCKNE MYSTERIES

DEAD WOOD (John Rockne Mystery #1)

HARD ROCK (John Rockne Mystery #2)

COLD JADE (John Rockne Mystery #3)

LONG SHOT (John Rockne Mystery #4)

EASY PREY (John Rockne Mystery #5)

BODY BLOW (John Rockne Mystery #6)

THE WADE CARVER THRILLERS

MOLLY (Wade Carver Thriller #1)

SUGAR (Wade Carver Thriller #2)

ANGEL (Wade Carver Thriller #3)

THE WALLACE MACK THRILLERS

THE KILLING LEAGUE (Wallace Mack Thriller #1)

THE MURDER STORE (Wallace Mack Thriller #2)

FINDERS KILLERS (Wallace Mack Thriller #3)

THE MARY COOPER MYSTERIES

DEATH BY SARCASM (Mary Cooper Mystery #1)

MURDER WITH SARCASTIC INTENT (Mary Cooper Mystery #2)

GROSS SARCASTIC HOMICIDE (Mary Cooper Mystery #3)

THE CIRCUIT RIDER (WESTERNS)

THE CIRCUIT RIDER (Circuit Rider #1)

KILLER'S DRAW (Circuit Rider #2)

THE RAY MITCHELL THRILLERS

THE RECRUITER

KILLING THE RAT

HEAD SHOT

STANDALONE THRILLERS:

KILLER GROOVE (Rockne & Cooper Mystery #1)

BEER MONEY (Burr Ashland Mystery #1)

TO FIND A MOUNTAIN (A WWII Thriller)

BOX SETS:

AMES TO KILL

GROSSE POINTE PULP

GROSSE POINTE PULP 2

TOTAL SARCASM

WALLACE MACK THRILLER COLLECTION

SHORT STORIES:

THE GARBAGE COLLECTOR

BULLET RIVER

SCHOOL GIRL

HANGING CURVE

SCALE OF JUSTICE

FREE BOOKS AND MORE

**Would you like a FREE copy
of my story BULLET RIVER and the
chance
to win a free Kindle?**

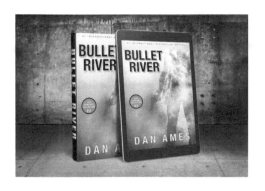

**Then sign up for the DAN AMES BOOK
CLUB:**

AUTHORDANAMES.COM

Made in United States
Troutdale, OR
10/12/2023

13639027R00322